# Rapture
# &
# Rogue

By

## Sydney Canyon

2015

**Rapture & Rogue** © 2015 Sydney Canyon
**Triplicity Publishing, LLC**

**ISBN-13: 978-0996242981**
**ISBN-10: 0996242988**

Printed in the United States of America
First Edition – 2015

Cover Design: Triplicity Publishing, LLC
Interior Design: Triplicity Publishing, LLC
Edited by: Jessica Roth - Triplicity Publishing, LLC

# Acknowledgements

Special thanks to my amazing and wonderful editor, Jessica. Your expertise made this story that much better.

# Dedication

To my wife:
Each chapter is small part in the book of life that I'm
fortunate enough to share with you.

# *Chapter 1*

A big, American Moving Company truck with red and blue block letters pulled away from the curb in front of the large brownstone and puttered down the street.

Taren Rauley swept her long, light-brown curls over her shoulder and tore her hazel eyes away from the window, sighing when she focused on the pile of boxes the delivery truck had just dropped off.

"I still can't believe my car won't be here for two days. I should've just driven it," she muttered as she began unpacking the nearest box.

"That's silly. Why would we drive two cars from San Diego to Chicago?" her boyfriend replied with a smile, pushing his dark-framed glasses back up his nose as he bent to pick up the box marked 'bedroom.'

Taren watched him walk down the hall. Ken reminded her a little bit of Matt Damon, except a nerdy, bookworm version. His dark brown hair was kept neat and just long enough to comb, and it was starting to show more and more gray on the sides, despite his age. He was 33, only a few years older than Taren. He wasn't very big for a man, standing at only five foot eight with the slim build of a morning jogger. Taren stood eye-to-eye with him when she wore three inch heels.

Focusing back on the project at hand, Taren went back to unpacking the kitchen. She hated moving across the country, but Ken received a promotion with his company that he couldn't turn down. Taren quit her job at a small accounting firm to move with him. She'd met Ken when she took on his company as a new client two years ago, and they had been together ever since. Taren hadn't been looking for a relationship, but Ken seemed to fit neatly into all of the little boxes she'd checked off in her head. He was genuinely nice, compassionate, book smart, and as loyal as a day is long. They'd moved in together after nine months.

"This is smaller than our apartment in San Diego, but at least it's furnished," Ken muttered as he entered the living area to get another box.

Taren mumbled in agreement without looking up. The apartment was actually the second floor of a four-story brownstone in an area close to the nightlife and downtown.

The front door opened to a small hallway, with bedroom and kitchen on the right. The hallway ended in a combination living and dining room.

The apartment was about eleven-hundred square feet and recently remodeled. A black leather couch and matching chair sat in the living area with dark brown tables. A flat screen TV hung over the corner fireplace. The small, four-person dining set had a matching dark brown frame with a glass top. The queen-sized furniture in the master bedroom was the same dark wood. The walls were a light shade of burnt orange with cream colored trim.

Taren finished setting up their coffee pot, toaster oven, and utensils. Then, she moved on to the next box, labeled 'dishes and cups.' She hated packing and unpacking, especially knowing the apartment wasn't permanent. Ken's company had paid the first six months rent in advance as part of the job offer. That way, they'd have time to look around and get the feel of the city before buying something. He'd sold Taren on the idea of exploring the real estate market in the new city. They sold their old furnishings to a friend, watched the movers pack their boxes into the truck, put her car on a shipping trailer, and headed across the country in Ken's compact SUV with their possessions stuffed in the back.

"I was thinking maybe we could go check out the area and get a real deep dish pizza."

Taren laughed, knowing he'd rather eat pizza than anything else.

"It seemed so much easier packing everything up," he sighed, plopping down on the couch and scratching the back of his head.

"It always does," she replied, sitting down next to him.

Ken wrapped his arm around and kissed her temple. "So, pizza?"

"We might as well. These boxes are going to take the rest of the day anyway. I can't believe we got here quicker than our stuff and my car," she sighed, running her fingers through her beautiful, wavy curls. "I can't even start looking for a job until I get my car." She'd hated quitting her job, but with her qualifications, she'd find another one easily.

Ken shrugged. "I know, honey. It'll be fine."

Taren kissed his lips and put her hand on his thigh as she pushed off the couch. "Where's the pizza place?" she asked as she headed into the bedroom to change clothes. She checked herself in the mirror. Her tanned skin contrasted nicely against the white cutoff shorts and pale green tank top she was wearing. She was going to miss sunny, southern California.

"This is Chicago. I figured we'd ride around until we found one. They're probably on every corner," he replied, tucking his light-yellow polo neatly into the waistband of his jeans.

\*\*\*

Later that evening, they finally finished all of the unpacking and headed to the bedroom. Ken was usually pretty quick in bed and smaller than average, but he was always attentive to Taren's needs, which made for a comfortable sex life. She thought about the reasons she loved him as he kissed her goodnight and curled up next to her. He was a compassionate, gentle person, who fumbled with romance, but made up for it in other ways.

# *Chapter 2*

A week after the move, Taren received a call with a job offer for major accounts manager with a prestigious accounting firm. She stared at the phone, in shock.

"Are you there, Ms. Rauley?"

"Yes. Sorry, we must have a bad connection," Taren fibbed.

"Oh. Anyway, we'd like you to start on Monday. Do you have any questions?"

"No. Thank you so much. I'm looking forward to it," Taren replied, and hung up. She ran around the apartment in her bare feet, a pair of short, cotton shorts, and the thin, low-rise tank top she'd worn to bed, even though it was three in the afternoon. "Yes!" she squealed and fist-pumped the air, before grabbing her phone to call Ken and give him the good news.

"That's great, babe! We should go out tonight to celebrate," he said.

"I think you're right," she answered.

\*\*\*

Ken asked around before leaving the office and many of his co-workers said an upscale cocktail bar called Rapture was the place to go. Taren dressed to the nines in a sleeveless, black, cocktail dress with a V in the front, showing off a hint of her perky cleavage, and strappy heels. Ken decided not to wear the coat and tie he'd worn to work, choosing to wear just the dark blue slacks and light blue button-down instead. He opened the first two buttons, allowing the collar on his white undershirt to be seen.

"This is different," Ken murmured as they walked through the doors of the high-end cocktail lounge.

There were bars along each side of the room with a stage in the far back, where a jazz band played softly. High-top tables were scattered around both bar areas with booths and couch and coffee table style seating in the middle. They made their way to the bar on the left, and Ken ordered a glass of red wine for each of them.

"It was twenty-five dollars for these," Ken squeaked, turning to hand Taren her glass.

"Wow," she replied. The bar wasn't full, but it was early. Everyone was fashionably dressed and the décor was modern with a lot of black, brushed stainless steel, and mirrors. "This place looks like something you'd see in Los Angeles," she added.

"Yeah, or maybe New York City. This must be where the rich people hang out," he replied. "Come on. I see an open table."

Taren followed as they made their way to one of the tables in the middle. She sat down and sipped her wine.

"The drinks are a little pricy, but I like the atmosphere," Ken said. The lighting was dim, but bright enough to see the fine artwork on the walls. The music permeated the air, but didn't drown out table conversation.

"It's a nice place," Taren agreed as she looked around the room. She froze, feeling a shiver crawl up her spine when her eyes landed on a woman in a corner booth with two suggestively dressed women snuggled up against either side of her. She had short, messy black hair, a flawless tan complexion and piercing blue eyes that were boring a hole through Taren. She quickly pulled her gaze away, gulping nearly half of her wine in one sip as she tried to focus on Ken.

"I'm going to find the restroom. Do you need anything?" Ken asked as he pulled her hand up and kissed the back of it before standing up.

Taren smiled and shook her head.

As soon as Ken walked away, a waiter stopped next to her table and set a drink in front of her. Taren didn't need to taste it to know it was a gin and tonic. She squeezed her eyes shut and swallowed the lump in her throat as the dark-haired woman from the corner booth slid into the seat across from her.

"I don't drink gin anymore," Taren murmured, avoiding the intense blue eyes staring at her.

The woman across from her laughed lightly. "You sure drank it in college," she said with a hint of arrogance in her voice.

"A lifetime ago," Taren sighed.

"I don't think five years constitutes a lifetime," the woman replied.

"It does for me." Taren finally pulled her eyes up to look at the woman across from her. "What do you want, Gi?" she asked, meeting her gaze.

"Miss me?" Gi asked with a casual smile.

"Hell no. What are you doing in Chicago anyway?"

"Surely you haven't forgotten all of our years of pillow talk. My family is here. This is where I grew up. What are you doing here, and who is the guy?"

"My boyfriend, Ken," Taren answered.

The woman laughed. "Does that make you his Barbie?"

"Fuck you," Taren spat.

"Oh, you used to do that. Quite well, I might add." Gi grinned. "It's odd, seeing you with a man. In all of the times we fucked, you were never interested in using a dildo, so you can't possibly enjoy being pounded by his dick."

"Gi, I don't care to see or talk to you. Please leave me alone," Taren said with a harsh tone in her voice.

"No, you're in my bar," Gi smirked.

"What?" Taren said.

"I own this bar."

"Oh, please," Taren huffed, shaking her head in disbelief. "Is there a poker table in the basement or something?"

"No." Gi smiled. "I left gambling when you left me." Her smile faded.

"Back to selling drugs?" she said sarcastically.

"No. I did dabble in guns and running call girls for a bit, but the crime boss life is a hassle." Gi gave her a smug look.

"You should go back to your whores. They look lonely," she sneered.

"Want to join me? They're pretty good in bed. Nothing like you." Gi wiggled her brows. "By the way, does *Ken* know how much you like eating pussy?" she taunted, grinning like a Cheshire cat.

Taren snapped, opening her mouth to yell at the woman across from her, when a man in a solid black suit stepped up to the table.

"Ms. Revisi, someone is here to see you," he said, nodding towards the front door, where a man stood, dressed in a dark grey, three piece suit. He had two younger men flanking him.

"Show them upstairs and tell Natasha their tab is on the house," Gi answered.

"Yes, ma'am."

Taren watched as the men were escorted through the bar and around the corner. They were all dressed in expensive suits and had the same dark hair and flawless olive skin that Gi had gotten from her Italian heritage.

"You're seriously washing money for the mob?" Taren screeched.

"Not so loud, tesoro," Gi murmured, using the Italian word for sweetheart.

Taren's chest burned when the pet name rolled off Gi's tongue like no time had passed. "Don't call me that, not anymore," she whispered heavily, turning her head away.

"Even after five years, you still get that look in your eyes. You're not fooling anyone but yourself," Gi stated softly before standing and walking away.

Taren refused to look up until Ken sat back down next to her.

"Where did this come from?" he asked, pointing to the drink on the table.

"A waiter dropped it off by mistake," Taren sighed.

Ken shrugged and took a sip. Taren watch him grimace.

"Gross!" he spat, sliding the glass to the other side of the table.

"I'm not feeling well. Do you think we could head home early?" Taren scrunched her face.

"Sure. Are you okay? You don't look well," he replied, noticing the color had drained from her face. It looked as though there were tears in her eyes.

"Yeah. The leftovers I ate were bad or something. I'm sorry."

"Don't apologize. This night was supposed to be for you. I'm sorry you feel bad. Do you want me to stop and get you something on the way home?"

"No. I'll be fine. I just want to go home and lie down. I guess you'll have to get dinner without me. Is that okay?"

"Don't worry about me. Come on." Ken stood and held his hand out to her.

Taren took his hand and they walked out of the bar together.

# *Chapter 3*

Taren woke in the middle of the night, drenched in sweat. She threw back the covers and slid out of bed, careful not to wake Ken who was sleeping soundly next to her. She quickly peeled out of her soaked tank top and replaced it with a new one from her drawer and walked out of the room.

Heavy rain drops pelted the windows from the storm outside, causing a steady rattle on the living room windows. Taren poured herself a cold glass of water and gathered her long, wavy curls and twisted them, holding her hair up to let the air conditioning caress the heat of her neck as she gulped the water down.

Afraid to wake Ken with her disturbed sleep, she stretched out on the sofa, allowing the coolness of the leather to soothe her back to sleep. She was barely out when the dreams invaded her conscience again.

\*\*\*

*Taren walked across the UCLA campus towards the row of campus apartments, the last of the sun's warmth kissing her skin before disappearing for the night. Long, wavy curls bounced along her back, hanging over her light blue tank top. She'd been invited to a party that evening and, as a newly moved-in freshman, she was looking forward to meeting new people.*

*"Hey! You made it," Christy said when she opened the door of the apartment. They'd met in one of their classes and had paired up as study buddies.*

*"Whose party is this?" Taren asked.*

*"Gi. Don't you know her?"*

*Taren shook her head.*

*"Really? Everyone knows Gi." Christy said, handing her a cup of beer from the keg. "Come on, I'll introduce you."*

*They walked towards the back of the apartment where Texas Hold'em and Black Jack tables were set up, each with a dealer. People gathered around them, holding cards and placing bets. Taren sipped her beer, grimacing at the bitter taste.*

*"You don't look like a beer drinker," a dark-haired girl with a sultry voice said, leaning close to her.*

*Taren turned to see the most beautiful, dark blue eyes she'd ever seen. "No, not really," she replied with a smile. "Do you know if there is anything else?"*

*"Come on," the girl said, holding her hand out.*

*Taren looked around for Christy, but she'd lost her once they got near the crowded tables. She shrugged and went with the girl who was tugging her hand. She was maybe two inches taller than Taren, and had short black hair that stuck out in all directions, wild and carefree. She was dressed in an old, thin t-shirt that clung to the small curves of her toned torso and worn blue jeans with a few holes in them.*

*There was an array of choices, as well as a dozen mixers, lining the kitchen counter.*

*"Is this your place?" Taren asked.*

*"No. I just supply the gambling," the girl answered. Taren nodded.*

*"Where shall we start?" the girl asked. "Are you even old enough to drink?" she teased.*

*"I'm old enough for a lot of things," Taren replied with a cocky grin.*

*"My kind of girl." She winked as she opened all the liquor bottles. "Stick your finger in each one and give it a taste. Stop when you find something you like."*

*Taren slid up next to her. She pushed her index finger down in the bottle of Tanqueray Gin, turning it upside down to coat the appendage. Then, she slipped it into her mouth, sucking the bitter flavor and swirling her tongue around before slowly pulling it free.*

*She was about to try the next bottle when Christy appeared.*

*"There you are. I see you've met Gi," Christy said to Taren and smiled up at the dark-haired girl next to her. "We're headed out of here. Brandon's out of money," she sighed, shaking her head. "I don't know why you keep letting him play when you know he loses every time."*

*"Maybe he should stop gambling the money his parents send him. Just a thought," Gi said. She winked at Taren and held her hand out. "Gianna Revisi, but most people just call me Gi."*

*"Taren Rauley," she replied, feeling the other girl's warm hand in hers once again.*

*"It was nice meeting you. I'm sure I'll see you around." She grinned and headed out of the kitchen.*

*"Do you want us to give you a ride back to the dorm?" Christy asked.*

*"Nah, I think I'll stick around a little longer."*

*"Be careful at those tables. Gi's dealers are better than Vegas."*

*"I will," Taren laughed.*

***

*A year later, Taren was sitting on the couch in her apartment, studying for an exam when the lock on the door clicked. She set her book on the coffee table as the door swung open. She stood and met the dark-haired intruder with a deep, searing kiss. She ran her hands under the thin leather jacket to caress Gi's small breasts.*

*Gi bumped the door closed and Taren shoved her back against it. She ran her hands under Taren's short shorts, squeezing her ass cheeks. "Someone missed me," Gi murmured against the lips that were teasing her with succulent kisses.*

*"You know I did," Taren answered, running her hand under the waistband of Gi's loose-fitting jeans, pressing her fingers into the wetness she knew was waiting for her.*

*"I was only gone an hour," Gi panted as she wiggled out of her jacket. "You know we have three parties tonight. I had to make sure everything was set up. Besides, you need to study," she said, grabbing Taren and pushing her back towards the couch.*

*Taren squealed playfully as she landed on her back with Gi on top of her.*

*"I don't think you studied at all," Gi chided, pinning her down.*

*"Yes, I did," Taren laughed.*

*"Uh huh. You need to get your degree so I can be a housewife one day," Gi chuckled.*

*"No. I'm going to be the housewife. That's why I hooked up with a criminal mastermind who is swindling all of the UCLA students out of their tuition money with her gambling racket,"* Taren said mocking Gi's current line of work.

Gi rolled her eyes.

*"Besides, you're in your senior year and you want to do the two year master's program. I think that qualifies me as housewife,"* Taren teased.

*"Either way, your beautiful, sexy, good looks aren't going to get you anywhere with Professor Tutwiler. She's straight as a board and probably hasn't had her legs parted in two decades."*

*"I know. I'm meeting with my study group later to go over the mid-term review she gave us."*

*"In that case…"* Gi smiled seductively and bent to suck Taren's braless nipple through her thin tank top.

Taren groaned, pushing her chest into Gi's mouth.

Gi kept her pinned with one hand as she worked her hand down Taren's body, sliding under her panty-less shorts and through the wet folds, circling her clit like prey before pushing deep inside her. Taren writhed back and forth under Gi as her body gave way to the impending orgasm. Gi kissed her passionately until the last wave had subsided.

*"You think you're hot shit, don't you?"* Taren panted with a smile.

Gi grinned like a Cheshire cat.

Taren lurched forward, dumping Gi onto the floor. She pounced before the dark-haired woman could get up.

*"Oh, I don't think so."* Taren bit her lower lip and slid down Gi's body, opening the button and zipper of her jeans when she reached it.

*Gi watched as Taren pulled the waistband of her pants down and buried her face between her legs, licking and sucking with excitement.*

*"Mmmm," Gi moaned as she ran her hand through the curly waves that fanned over her thigh. She rose up to meet Taren, matching her stroke for stroke until she lost control.*

*Taren kissed Gi's thighs and pushed her long hair to her back as she crawled up the body underneath her. Their lips met in a feverish kiss.*

*"I love you, Gi," Taren whispered, looking down into those deep blue eyes as she affectionately brushed the messy hair off Gi's forehead.*

*"I love you too, tesoro," Gi smiled and kissed her softly.*

\*\*\*

*Three years later, Taren was looking forward to graduation, when she got a call from a classmate.*

*"I didn't see you at the tournament last night," Chelsea said.*

*"I was studying. These finals are going to make me crazy." Taren hadn't been to a tournament or poker party in the last two months. She'd heard rumors that the school was trying to crack down on the illegal gambling ring and she was too close to graduating to let anything get in her way.*

*"I haven't seen Gi in forever. I guess she's gotten too big to hang around the tables anymore," Chelsea laughed.*

*"Yeah, something like that."*

16

*"Anyway, let her know the mayor's son was there last night and my boyfriend said he saw him at the last one, too. I'm not sure if she knows that."*

*"Oh, wow. Okay. I'll see you in class tomorrow."* Taren hung up and walked into the bathroom.

Gi climbed out of the shower and grinned at Taren as she toweled off. *"You could've joined me."*

*"When were you going to tell me Mayor Jackson's son was gambling in your tournaments?"*

*"He is?"* Gi shrugged.

*"You know the school is investigating. Why the fuck are you expanding now?"* Taren growled. *"Do you want to go to prison? Do you want* me *to go to prison?"*

*"Calm down, tesoro."* Gi said. *"I have it under control. The school is no closer to me now than they were when I started."*

*"This is crazy, Gi. When I first met you, this was all for entertainment and a few bucks on the side. Now, you're running an illegal gambling racket that has gone way off campus and gotten so big you have no idea who's sitting at the tables anymore."*

*"I didn't see you complaining when the money I made paid for cruises and Spring Break vacations down in Cancun and Cozumel,"* Gi countered.

*"Damn it, Gi. This is serious. I can't go to prison with you. I'm out."*

*"Out? What the fuck does that mean?"*

*"I've spent the last four years with you, as your girlfriend and as your bookkeeper. I'm done. This power trip, criminal ring leader, or whatever the hell it is you have going on in your head that keeps encouraging you to delve deeper and deeper into this business, it's eating away at you. All you do is eat, sleep, and breathe this operation.*

*It's like the only ambition you have now is being a crime boss. I don't think you have any intention of ever stopping. I'm not going to stick around to watch it ruin you. Find someone else to do your accounting."*

*Gi said nothing as she watched Taren toss her belongings into a duffle bag.*

*"I love you with all of my heart, but it's over. You're not dragging me down with you when this blows up. They're coming, Gi. Everyone knows it and as smart as you are, I can't believe you don't see it." Taren moved to the closet outside of the bathroom and began filling up the bag with her clothes.*

*"Seriously? You're leaving me because you think I'm going to get busted? I'm very good at what I do. No one is coming near me, and for the record, I know who is at every single table and how much they win or lose. You do, too, because you've been keeping the books for three years. No one goes to my tables if I don't want them there." Gi explained. "I can't believe you think I'd let something happen to you."*

*"Not intentionally. But you can't stop it if it happens," she said sadly. "Goodbye, Gianna."*

*Taren wiped the tears from her face as she placed her key on the kitchen counter and walked away without looking back. Leaving had been the hardest thing she'd ever done. Walking away from the person she knew she was meant to be with was like cutting her own wrists and watching the blood pool on the floor, but she had to get away from that lifestyle. Gi was heading down a treacherous path and no matter how many times Taren tried to change her course, Gi continued on. Taren couldn't watch her tumble and fall. She loved her too much to see her hit the bottom.*

\*\*\*

Taren awoke again in a fit, nearly falling off the couch as tears ran down her cheeks. "Damn you, Gi," she whispered harshly. Her thoughts drifted back to the bar.

Sitting across from her tonight, Gi had looked so different. Gone was the cocky kid in threadbare jeans and worn, 80s logo t-shirts who didn't have a care in the world. The person sitting at her table was a very confident woman. Gi had grown up, trimmed her hair much shorter, and exchanged her casual wardrobe for a fitted Armani suit. She looked every bit on the outside the sexy and dangerous mobster she was on the inside.

# *Chapter 4*

A week later, Taren had settled into her new position - accounting manager for Nicholson and Brass, a firm downtown. She'd taken over for a man who had retired, so she was handed his accounts. She'd decided to start with her largest: a multi-million dollar holdings company called R&R Enterprises.

After a quick call to the company office, she had a meeting set up with the President of the company for the following morning. She hadn't gone through the portfolio yet. She was trying to get in touch with her top clients to do a meet and greet before looking over their accounts. Still, she was shocked that the President of R&R wanted to meet her at Rapture and equally surprised when the secretary on the phone said the bar was open during the day for business meetings only. She wasn't exactly happy about going back there, but surely Gi wouldn't be around during the morning hours. The woman had never risen before ten a.m. the entire time they were together.

\*\*\*

Taren tossed her briefcase onto the dining table and headed into the bedroom to get out of her heels and skirt suit. Ken was just stepping out of the shower when she walked through the closet to the bathroom.

"You're home early," she said, slightly surprised. She hadn't seen his compact SUV parked along the curb out front.

"Yeah. I have to fly to Dallas in the morning to oversee an acquisition," he replied, standing near the sink with a towel tied around his waist. He put his glasses on and finger-combed his short hair while looking in the mirror. He wasn't a large guy by any means, but he was physically fit and had a thin amount of light brown hair in the middle of his chest.

"That sucks." Taren pursed her lips and sighed. "I haven't been to the gym all week. I'm too damn tired when I get out of the office."

"I figured you were going every morning." Ken turned around to face her as he leaned back against the sink counter.

"No. We've had early meetings all week and afternoon sessions with the tech people. They changed the entire computer system over last week, so everyone has to be trained on it this week. I was finally able to sit down at my desk today and start contacting my clients. I set up meetings for the rest of this week with my top five accounts." She pulled the dark red blouse over her head, revealing a lacy black bra and matching panties. "Get this," she added. "The president of my top account wants to meet me at Rapture tomorrow."

Ken furrowed his brow. "That bar we went to?"

Taren nodded. "They're open during the day for business meetings."

"Weird. Who is the client?"

"R&R Enterprises. The office manager's name is Pete Cabrera, but his secretary is the one who booked the meeting at Rapture."

Ken stepped forward, wrapping his arms around her waist. "Why don't get grab an early dinner since we're both home? I need to pack and get to bed early. My flight leaves at six in the morning."

"Dinner sounds good." She leaned back and smiled. "How about that Chinese place down the road?"

"That's fine with me." He kissed her cheek and pulled away to go get dressed.

\*\*\*

The next morning, Taren kicked herself for not looking over the portfolio of her largest client. After dinner, she'd gone to bed with Ken and fell asleep after their quick lovemaking. She didn't wake again until her alarm went off the next morning, leaving her only an hour to get ready and head to her meeting.

She arrived a little early, so she pulled the file from her briefcase and began skimming over it. R&R Enterprises was a parent company and had been in business for three years. Upon further reading, Taren noticed the subsidiary companies were Rapture Cocktail Lounge LLC and Rogue Night Club LLC. She raised an eyebrow and flipped a few pages back to the organizational chart. At the top of the page was the last name she'd expected to see. She slammed the file closed and prepared to leave, not wanting to go through with the meeting after all.

"Leaving so soon?" Gi asked, pulling out the chair across from Taren and sitting down with two cups of coffee in her hand. She slid one to Taren.

Taren's chest tightened at the sound of the familiar voice. "I had no idea you were my client," Taren growled, shaking her head. She was pissed at herself for not reading

22

the file and so infuriated that Gi remembered how she liked her coffee that she refused to drink it, despite how enticing it smelled.

"Is that going to be a problem? I'm as surprised as you are. What happened to Ronald?"

"He retired and I took over his accounts. I'll give your portfolio to one of the senior members when I get back to the office." Taren moved to get up.

"So, that's it then?"

Taren looked at the deep blue eyes staring back at her. "What do you want from me, Gi? I'm not doing this. I've been trying so damn hard to forget I saw you, to forget you're right here in the same goddamn city."

"And this is easy for me?" Gi spat. "You walked out on me, Taren. Not the other way around. I'm the one who should be pissed you're here."

Taren tore her eyes away.

"Maybe I should just drop Nicholson and Brass," Gi sighed. It had taken her over a year to get comfortable with her accountant, and even then she didn't give him full access.

"They'll drop you when they find out you're laundering money for the mob!" Taren fired back.

Gi laughed softly. "You think so highly of me."

"How else do you own all of this? And don't give me some bullshit story."

"If there is one thing I'm good at, it's business management. You should know that better than anyone."

"Yeah, illegal business!"

"I always liked your feisty side." Gi grinned.

"I'm not getting involved in whatever you're doing here, Gi. Not this time." Taren shook her head.

"I bet you haven't read that file. If you had, you wouldn't be sitting here attacking me about our past, which you were equally involved in, by the way."

"You and I..." Taren murmured, trailing off. "We're not the reason I'm here," she said, changing her tone. If her firm lost one of their largest accounts, she'd lose her job and possibly her reputation as a large portfolio accountant. As much as she hated it, she had to figure out a way to work with Gi. If the account looked good, she'd only have to see her once a quarter anyway.

Gi sipped her coffee as she watched the emotions play across Taren's face. Defeated, Taren turned her hazel eyes back to her.

"I'll go through your portfolio this week. If I find anything, I'm out, Gi."

"Fair enough."

"I'm serious."

"So am I. If something isn't right, I want to know about it right away." Gi finished her coffee. "How's Ken?" she asked sarcastically.

"My personal life is off limits," Tarenwarned.

"You don't have to say anything. Your eyes do it for you," Gi said, reaching into the inside pocket of her dark grey jacket and removing one of her business cards. She wrote her cell phone number on the back and slid the card across the table.

Taren watched her walk away, then shoved the card into the file folder and left the bar.

"If you're still walking that line, Gi, I'm going to find out," she murmured, placing her head in her hands before sliding behind the wheel of her car.

\*\*\*

Later that night, Taren was sitting with the entire R&R portfolio sprawled out on the dining room table. She started with the tax records from the first year and worked her way forward, noting every change within the business from employment W2's to supply statements.

When Ken called later that evening to see how her day had gone, Taren brushed over the meeting with Gi. Instead, she focused on him and his trip, which kept him talking for over an hour.

She'd finally fallen asleep after one a.m. with the file next to her pillow.

\*\*\*

Taren was still working on the R&R portfolio when Ken returned from his business trip on Saturday. She barely got up from the dining table to greet him.

"Is everything okay?" Ken asked before going to unpack.

"Of course." She kissed his cheek. "I'm just swamped with this account. The president of the company had some issues with the previous guy, so I need to make sure I know this company inside and out."

"Don't work too hard." He said, wrapping his arms around her. "I was thinking maybe we could go to the Art Institute. I read about it on the plane. It's supposed to be really great," he added as he carried his suitcase into the bedroom.

Taren sighed. She loved Ken and found his nerdy side appealing, but her mind was elsewhere. She couldn't be mad at him for wanting to do something he found fun and exciting. No, her animosity was towards the one person who seemed to still be able to capture all of her attention, no matter how hard she fought it. *Damn you, Gianna Revisi!* she thought.

"Well?" Ken questioned, stepping back into the living room.

"Yes." Taren smiled brightly. "I want to get this account off my mind. Give me a few minutes to get ready." She kissed him and jogged into the bedroom.

Ken was taken aback when Taren returned to the living room. She was dressed casually in short, khaki shorts with a tight, light-yellow tank top and sandals. Her long, wavy curls had a natural windblown look as they fell over each breast. A pair of aviator sunglasses dangled from one hand.

"You can take the girl out of California, but you can't take California out of the girl," Ken said with a nerdy grin.

\*\*\*

Taren and Ken spent three and a half hours walking around the museum, looking at photographs, sculptures, and paintings from various time periods and cultures. They'd even taken in an early dinner at one of the cafés before leaving. Taren realized she hadn't thought about Gi or her company the entire time, but as soon as they arrived back at the apartment, the Italian femme fatale was on her mind once again. Gi had been her Achilles' heel; the addiction she'd tried so hard to let go of, and the lover she thought she'd never be able to live without. It had taken her well over a year to get past her life with Gi and meeting Ken had been a godsend. He was the final piece of the delicate new life she'd built.

\*\*\*

"I hate traveling for work," Ken murmured, cuddling Taren close. They were laying in bed, watching reruns on the Discovery Channel.

Taren smiled and placed her hand on his face. "Traveling is part of the job. You knew that when you took the promotion."

"I know, but it takes me away from you," he added, kissing the top of her head, then her cheek, moving to initiate sex.

Taren's mind was miles away from the bedroom. "I'm really tired," she yawned truthfully. "But…" she trailed off, sliding her hand under the covers to give him a hand job.

Ken enjoyed the feeling of her warm hand wrapped around his manhood, but pushed her away. "It's okay. We don't have to if you're tired. I'm just happy to be home with you."

# Chapter 5

After spending four full days going through the R&R financials, Taren found something that didn't quite add up. She hadn't really been sure what she was looking for to begin with, except something to prove Gi was lying about giving up her criminal past. She nearly jumped up and down screaming with joy, until she realized what she'd found was a discrepancy for transactions that actually had nothing to do with the bar or the night club, meaning it was possibly something Gi knew nothing about. *Damn it*, she thought.

The last thing Taren had wanted to do was actually have to work with Gi regarding her account. She'd only decided to keep the account because the notion of proving Gi was lying to her would be worth it in the end and she'd be free once again from the connection that was pulling her back down memory road. Taren honestly didn't believe that Gianna Revisi would give up being a criminal mastermind, especially after she'd made a life of it and chosen that life over her. She needed to prove to herself that Gi hadn't changed at all.

Taren checked and double-checked the discrepancy before making the dreaded phone call. Gi was out of the office, but her assistant booked a meeting for that afternoon. She hung up the phone and stared at the backwards slanted, handwritten numbers Gi had scrawled on her business card. Her writing had gotten a little more legible over the last five years, but it was still distinctively Gi.

Taren added the number to the contacts on her cell phone, and then tucked the card into the top drawer of her desk. She brushed her wavy curls over her shoulder and pushed her chair back as she stood up. She had two hours to kill before the meeting that would end her work day, so she decided to go grab some lunch and hopefully keep her mind from rolling back to Gi.

*** 

"I'm glad you called," Ken smiled, kissing Taren's cheek. "It's nice to meet for lunch."

Taren nodded in agreement. She'd chosen to invite him to lunch with the hope that seeing him would clear her head, but it hadn't worked. She kept thinking about her upcoming meeting.

"I may be a little late getting home. I have a meeting with my top client this afternoon."

"No problem. I'm going to gym after work anyway."

"I went this morning," Taren replied. "I couldn't believe how many people were there. I had to wait in line to get on the elliptical machine, so I wound up cycling instead."

"That sucks," Ken said as he handed the waiter his bankcard to pay the bill.

"If you don't mind waiting, I'll pick up takeout on my way home."

"Sure." He smiled, pushing his glasses up before finishing off the last sip of tea in his glass. "Can you sign that slip when it comes back? I need to go to the restroom."

Taren nodded.

\*\*\*

Rapture was open for regular business and had a few people sitting at the bars on both sides when Taren walked inside. She subconsciously ran her hand down the front of her black slacks, removing imaginary wrinkles. Then, she looked down, making sure the buttons of her light-blue, form-fitting blouse were fastened as she stepped up to the bar on the left. The blouse was new and the last thing she needed was to have the buttons over her breasts pop open in front of Gi. She saw herself in the mirror behind the array of liquor bottles, noticing the expanse of naked skin showing above her hidden cleavage. The space under her collarbones looked empty, like something was missing. She hadn't worn a necklace in five years, but today a feeling of emptiness blossomed at the sight.

"What can I get you?" the bartender asked with a smile.

Taren pushed her hair to her back, allowing it to fan over her left shoulder. She set her briefcase on the stool next to her and pushed her three-quarter sleeves up. "Ms. Revisi is expecting me," she said.

He pointed to his left. "There's a side door around the corner. You'll find the elevator through there."

\*\*\*

With Gi, Taren had always told it like it was, no holds barred, but for some reason, she was nervous, standing in the elevator as it rose one floor to the R&R offices. She held her breath as the doors slid open.

Burgundy carpet covered the small room and a high-countered reception desk sat directly across from the elevator, with a few lobby-style chairs in front of it. The walls were solid black with modern décor along both sides. "R&R" was painted in large silver letters behind the reception desk.

"Good afternoon, ma'am."

The young woman at the desk was on some kind of platform, as she was sitting and still able to see over the large counter.

"Taren Rauley with Nicholson and Brass Accounting," Taren said. "I have an appointment with Ms. Revisi."

"Ms. Revisi should return any minute. She asked that you wait in her office," the receptionist said as she stepped down and walked around the counter.

Taren followed her down the only hallway to the door at the end. The young woman opened the door and flipped the light on. The room was large with the same dark red carpet and black walls as the rest of the building. A large metal desk with a glass top sat opposite the entrance with a large floor-to-ceiling, tinted window behind it.

A matching bookcase was along the left side wall, and a black leather couch was against the right wall under an array of black and white photos. Taren walked in and took a seat on the couch. The chairs by the desk looked uncomfortable. She placed her briefcase next to her and removed the files.

Gi walked through the door a few minutes later, dressed in a black pantsuit with a black, button-down blouse. She looked slightly disheveled, hair sticking out in all directions, reminding Taren of the way she used to wear it.

"I knew you'd be back to see me." Gi grinned. "Sorry I'm late. My schedule got a little distorted this afternoon," she added, looking at the beautiful woman sitting on her couch.

"So did your clothing," Taren huffed, mad that she'd been kept waiting while Gi had a tryst with God knows who.

Gi raised an eyebrow and looked down at herself. Then, she turned to one of the pieces of art on the wall, a collage of mirrors. She laughed at her reflection, and noted she was in serious need of a haircut.

"If you think I spent the last hour with a sexy woman wrapped around me, you're sadly mistaken. I was at a meeting downtown and drove across the city with the top down. It's a beautiful day," Gi said, walking towards the couch.

"There's no need to make excuses for me. I don't care what or who you do," Taren stated matter-of-factly. "I found something in your records that doesn't add up and I need to confirm it with you."

"What is it?" Gi asked, ignoring the jab as she sat down next to her with the briefcase between them. "Everything is legal and legitimate with this company, so whatever it is, it's not supposed to be there."

Taren ignored her and laid the bank statements out on the table, along with the ledger records. "You've been writing checks, according to the ledger, and they should be going into these accounts, but none of the money has been deposited."

"What?" Gi grabbed the papers and began looking them over. "I'm not laundering money for the mob."

"That's not what this is. These checks are either being cashed or the money is being redistributed elsewhere within the company," Taren added. "If it's going back into the company, I need to know where so I can balance the ledger."

"I have no idea." Gi shrugged. "If someone's stealing from me…" she trailed off.

"Did you personally sign these checks?"

"Sure. I sign checks all the time, but I don't research every single check before signing it." She smacked the table in disgust. "Damn it!" she snapped. "How far back does this go? How much is missing?"

"I don't know. I haven't gotten very far," Taren replied nervously. She knew what Gi was capable of when someone stole from her. One night when they'd calculated the earnings for one of the gambling parties, the numbers didn't match. When Gi went to collect, the guy tried to say he had given her everything. When she found out he'd stolen two-thousand dollars from her, she broke his fingers. That was the only time Taren had seen Gi's fierce, Italian side come out.

"I'll figure out what's going on. Can I keep these?" Gi asked, holding the ledger copies and bank statements.

"Yes." Taren nodded. Either Gi was pissed that her neatly hidden illegal business had somehow popped up on the radar, or she truly had a thief in her company. Taren had known her so well and had been able to read each emotion as it crossed her face, but she wasn't sure she wanted to know the truth, so she turned away from the blue eyes looking back at her. "Let me know if you figure it out so I can adjust the ledger for the quarter," she muttered as she left.

As soon as Taren walked outside, she took a long, deep breath. Even after five long years, that woman's eyes still bore her to the core. Seeing Gi again in the midst of her new life had cut her deep, spilling out the past that she'd tried desperately to let go of, and now, every time she saw her, it opened that wound all over again. *Why the hell can't I let her go? I walked away. I chose a new life!* She sighed heavily as she walked towards her car.

Taren tossed her briefcase into the passenger seat and started the car. Backing out, she noticed the convertible Audi parked between two larger SUVs. The license plate read: GR219, which stood for Gi's name and birthday. Taren shook her head and floored the gas pedal.

# *Chapter 6*

Over the next week, Taren familiarized herself with the rest of her accounts, meeting or calling every one of them, even the mundane ones at the bottom of her list, to introduce herself. She pushed Gianna Revisi and R&R Enterprises to the back of her mind.

She thought she was free of the past that had been haunting her dreams, until the night she closed her eyes and opened them again on a sandy beach with the sun beating down overhead and crystal clear, turquoise water in front of her.

*Taren watched Gi walk towards her, dripping wet from the warm Caribbean water. She was dressed in a black string bikini top that barely covered her small breasts and short, black board shorts. Her short hair was wet and sticking out in all directions. A tattoo in Italian script that read* "Una vita bella è quella che è vissuta al Massimo; *a beautiful life is one lived to the fullest," covered her left ribcage. Another,* "non fidarti di nessuno," *circled her left wrist like a bracelet: trust no one.*

*"Gi," Taren squealed when the woman stopped next to where she was lying on a beach towel and shook her hair like a wet dog. "You're getting me wet!"*

*"Isn't that the point?" Gi wiggled her eyebrows. She lowered herself onto the towel next to Taren.*

*Taren climbed on top of her, straddling her hips as she brushed her long, wavy curls to the side and leaned down, kissing Gi hard. "I love you so damn much, Gianna," she murmured.*

*"I love you too, tesoro. Happy anniversary," Gi replied.*

*"This has been the best two years of my life." Taren beamed, still straddling Gi. "I want to commemorate it. Let's do something crazy."*

*"I thought flying down to the Cayman Islands last minute was something crazy."*

*"I'm serious," Taren laughed. "I want to get a tattoo."*

*"Since when?" Gi asked. Taren had always said Gi's tattoo on her side was sexy, but only on her. She'd never mentioned wanting one herself.*

*"Since now." Taren pulled the front of her bikini bottoms down an inch. "I want 'tesoro' tattooed right here," she said, pointing to her left hipbone.*

*"Are you sure? It'll be there forever."*

*"Yes," Taren replied, leaning down to kiss her again, this time rubbing herself back and forth over Gi's crotch.*

*"We're going to get kicked off this beach if you keep that up," Gi murmured.*

*"Wouldn't be the first time," Taren grinned and bit her lower lip.*

\*\*\*

Taren opened her eyes and stared into the darkness, confused at her surroundings. Ken was snoring softly next to her. She threw the covers back, stood, and walked out of the bedroom. The microwave clock read 2:47 when she stepped into the kitchen to pour herself a glass of cold water. She took a long sip and placed the glass on the counter, then pulled the waistband of her panties down. The word "tesoro" was written in cursive inside her left hip. Taren ran her finger over the black curves and sighed before covering them back up. She reached for the water glass again, drinking the rest of it in one long sip.

As she made her way back to the bedroom, she thought about the first time Ken had seen her tattoo. She never thought anyone but Gi would ever see it, and in a way, it was something meant only for the two of them. When he asked about it, she lied and said she drank too much one night in college, woke up with it, and was thankful it wasn't Tweety Bird.

***

The next morning, Ken was sitting at the dining table, eating a bagel and drinking coffee when Taren walked out of the bedroom looking tousled.

"Did you sleep okay?" he asked.

"No."

"Is it that bed? It's a little harder than our old one."

"No...I don't know what it is," she lied, pouring herself a cup of coffee.

"Could be stress. You've been working like a dog."

"I'm just trying to get caught up. This firm puts their accountants under a lot of pressure with a hundred clients each. I need to get used to balancing my workload."

"I'm sure you're the best accountant there. Once you get a system going, they'll all want to model their work ethic after you," he said with a smile.

"Maybe." She smiled softly at him.

\*\*\*

Taren felt tired from lack of sleep and a long, boring day staring at a computer screen. She was about to call it quits and head to the gym when her desk phone rang. She looked at the clock, knowing she had to take the call.

"Taren Rauley," she answered.

"You sound cheery," the voice on the other end said.

"What do you want, Gi?" she sighed.

"Can you meet me this evening?"

"No." Taren palmed her forehead. "What for?" she asked with a sigh.

"I think I know what's going on with the missing money."

"Great. Then you don't need me."

"I want to look at everything again. I'm sure Mr. Barbie can wait an hour for you to play house," Gi said sarcastically.

"Funny," Taren mumbled. "Are you in the office?"

"Yes."

"I'll be there in twenty minutes," Taren said and hung up. She grabbed her briefcase and headed out the door.

\*\*\*

Rapture was starting to pick up an early evening crowd when Taren arrived. She walked to the elevator and took it up to the main offices. When the door opened, the receptionist told her Gi was in her office, so Taren headed down the hallway. The clack-clack sound of her heels was silenced by the thick carpet. She was just about to Gi's office door when an older man walked out, with two younger men behind him. They were all dressed to the nines in dark suits and Italian leather shoes. The older man had thinning, salt and pepper hair slicked back with gel. One of the men behind him looked like a younger version of himself and the other guy looked strikingly similar to Gi, but with brown eyes. Taren nodded politely as she passed them. The gentleman who looked like Gi gave her a long look and a sly grin. She ignored it and turned the door knob.

"Do you do this for all of your clients?" Gi asked from her position behind the desk when Taren stepped inside.

"What?"

"Appear at the drop of a hat, mad as a hornet and eager to work."

Taren raised an eyebrow and took a seat in front of Gi's desk as Gi pointed to one of the computers on her desk. Nine little screens showed various camera angles monitoring the bar and parking lot.

"I passed your mob friends in the hallway. Why don't you just come clean? You're doing something illegal and I found your paper trail."

. "The money isn't missing and I'm not doing anything illegal,"Gi pressed. "I'm expanding with a third company and the money was going to that, albeit the wrong way. I straightened everything out just now, actually."

"Great. You're in business with the mob. That's worse than laundering money!"

"Your fuse has gotten a lot shorter, tesoro," Gi sighed.

Taren's chest burned as the word rolled off Gi's lips. "You could've said all of this over the phone," she said, through gritted teeth.

"I know." Gi leaned back in her chair. "I asked you to come here so I could do this in person."

"Do what?" Taren asked, her voice thick with frustration.

"Either you really do hate me or you haven't had good sex in a very long time," Gi stated. "I don't think I've ever seen you wound this tight."

"What do you think?" Taren spat.

"Surely the latter." Gi grinned.

"I don't have time for this."

"Time for what?" Gi asked.

"Playing head games with you." Taren shook her head and sighed. "What do you want from me, Gi?"

"I want you to come work for me as the Financial Director of R&R."

"You're kidding me," Taren said, skeptical.

"No. I need someone handling the finances of this company so stupid shit like this doesn't happen again."

"Gi...I can't." Taren looked away.

"I think you'll find this well worth it," Gi replied, sliding a folded paper across the desk.

Taren opened the paper, swallowing the lump in her throat when she saw all of the zeros at the end of the lucrative salary. "This is...No. You and I...we're destructive together. It's unhealthy."

"This wasn't a ploy to get you back with me." Gi met her eyes. "Taren, you're unbelievably smart and you're wasting your talents at that shithole company."

"I can't, Gi," Taren murmured, pulling gaze away as she stood to leave.

"I'll be cutting ties with Nicholson and Brass when I fill this position, just so you know," Gi added.

Taren nodded and walked out of the office.

\*\*\*

Taren headed to a small dive bar near her house. A slow pop song was playing over the speakers when she sat on the stool. The piano-filled tune was familiar from the radio, but she didn't know the lyrics.

"What can I get for you?"

The woman behind the bar had pretty brown eyes and short blond hair, pulled to each side in pigtails. The natural, perky breasts poking up under her tight black tank top gave away her tender age.

"Gin and tonic," Taren murmured, feeling flattened.

The job offer from Gi had been lucrative, more than twice her current salary, but no higher than any other financial officer position, so Gi wasn't trying to buy her. Still, there was no way they could work together. When she'd left her criminal lover, Taren promised herself she'd never be involved with illegal activities, and she'd never see Gianna Revisi again.

The bartender set the drink in front of her and Taren took a long sip, reveling in the familiar taste. The past she'd tried to forget was so close she could feel it on her skin. Her life was so different now. Taren was more worried that she'd never be able to separate the past from the present once they entangled. She'd definitely noticed a difference in Gi during their brief meetings, but the younger Gi was haunting her dreams at night. Could she keep the two apart?

"Bad day at the office?" the bartender asked.

"You could say that," Taren replied, finishing the drink.

"Get you another?"

"No, thanks." Taren tossed some cash on the bar and walked out.

\*\*\*

Steam rose from takeout containers on the table as Taren walked into the apartment. She kicked off her heels and inhaled the aroma of Japanese Hibachi while walking towards her bedroom.

"Hey." Ken smiled, kissing her cheek. He was standing in the kitchen, gathering plates and silverware.

"Dinner smells divine." Taren's stomach rumbled as she began removing her blouse and skirt.

"How was your day?" Ken asked, walking up behind her and kissing her bare shoulder.

*Great, until my ex-girlfriend turned my world upside down.* "Fine. A little hectic at the end. You?" she answered, turning and kissing him before pulling on a pair of cotton shorts and a tank top.

"Pretty good. We're working on a new acquisition," he replied as they walked out of the bedroom together.

"Where's this one?"

"St. Louis. We still have a few weeks before everything is finalized, so I won't be traveling until then." He sat down and passed her the carton of rice.

"I see." She said, taking the container and pouring rice onto her plate.

"Paul and Cindy invited us for a night out this weekend," Ken stated, changing the subject as he added a soy sauce to his food.

"Really? Where?"

"Local nightclub," he replied, chewing a piece of steak.

Taren laughed. "You're not a nightclub person."

"Yeah, that's what I said, but it could be fun."

Taren shrugged. "Sure. I could use a change of scenery anyway."

"Great. I'll let him know tomorrow."

# *Chapter 7*

By Saturday, Taren had all but talked herself out of the job at R&R. She'd already told Gi the answer was no, yet it still weighed heavily on her mind. She tried to avoid all rational thoughts as she dressed for a night out with Ken and their new friends. She'd almost backed out when she found out they were going to Rogue, but the chances of Gi hanging around her nightclub on a Saturday night were fairly slim. Taren had a good feeling Rapture was more her scene these days.

"What do you think of this shirt?" Ken asked.

Taren turned around to see him. He was wearing black slacks and a shirt that was covered in a pattern of tiny black and white checkers. He looked more like he was going to church than a nightclub.

"It's fine. Is it new?"

"Yeah. I picked it up at the mall when I was looking for new running shoes." He added a belt to his ensemble and slipped into a pair of black oxford shoes with thick soles, before going into the bathroom to comb his short hair. He splashed on a bit of cologne and waited for Taren.

A few minutes later, Taren stepped out of the closet wearing a pair of black pants with a tight, sheer, black button-down that only had the middle two buttons fastened, leaving her chest and lower midriff bare. She completed the sexy outfit with a pair of black, open-toed sling-backs. Her long, wavy curls hung down her back and over her left shoulder.

"Wow," Ken beamed. "You look…hot."

Taren laughed and ran her hand down the center of his chest.

\*\*\*

Rogue had a good crowd inside when they arrived. Ken spotted Paul and Cindy next to the bar and ushered Taren over to them. A steady thump of bass with steamy lyrics played.

Taren and Cindy stood close and introduced themselves while the men ordered drinks.

"Do you come here often?" Taren asked.

"Only when we feel like cutting loose and dancing. This place is very popular and most nights, you can't get in the door unless you arrive early. In another two hours, it'll be wall-to-wall people."

"Wow," Taren replied, impressed.

"They don't have wine, so I ordered you the same thing he got for Cindy," Ken said loudly, handing Taren a drink.

"What is it?" she asked Cindy before taking a sip.

"Long Island Iced Tea. You'll love it, but it'll knock you on your ass," she cheered, clinking their glasses together.

"Lovely," Taren replied, with a laugh.

The small group moved to the end of the bar where they could watch the dance floor and sip their drinks. Watching the patrons on the dance floor reminded Taren of the club she and Gi used to frequent in college. They'd spent many nights dancing in each other's arms until they were kicked out, heading home to make love until sunrise. She shook the memories from her head when she felt someone touch her arm.

"Do you want to dance?" Ken asked.

Taren nodded and set the full drink on the bar, having never taken a sip. She wasn't much of a liquor drinker anymore and Long Islands had never been her favorite. The other couple followed them. Ken wasn't much of a dancer, but he tried. Paul and Cindy on the other hand, were all over each other, grinding to the bass like a pair of college kids. Taren danced close to Ken here and there, leaving plenty of space between them, which he preferred since he needed to see his feet to dance. When they'd first met, his nerd qualities were what had attracted her to him. He was so different and she liked that about him.

As the songs changed, the dance floor became more crowded, pushing the two couples away from each other. Taren got into the music, dancing like she'd never stop going clubbing. She moved her body with precision, rhythmically swaying and shaking her hips in a seductive motion. She'd nearly forgotten all about the other people she was with, until she felt a warm body close behind her. She backed up, thinking it was Ken, but as she pressed their bodies together, she realized she couldn't be more wrong. The sensation of a warm, female body sent a chill of excitement down her spine. Taren leaned back further, allowing herself to revel in the feeling of another woman against her. She never missed a step as their bodies melded together, their hips swaying in time.

A hand snaked around Taren's side, resting on her bare abdomen as warm breath tickled her neck. Taren put her hand over the one touching her skin and pushed it higher to her breast, forgetting her surroundings as the long-buried sensation of being touched by a woman came flooding back to her. The beat of music was lost as the two women moved to their own sultry rhythm like lovers meeting in the night. Taren ran her hand up the arm around her until she felt the short hair and light sheen of sweat on the base of the woman's neck. A soft moan escaped her lips as she tugged at the short hair.

"I knew you missed me," the woman whispered into her ear.

Taren's body stiffened before she jumped away and spun around to face her.

"Damn you, Gi!" she growled, staring at the sexy grin and deep blue eyes of the woman looking back at her.

"We're good together and you know it," Gi stated. She hadn't been trying to get her back, but seeing Taren on the dance floor had brought back memories and she couldn't help getting close to her, even if it was only for a minute.

"I'm with Ken," Taren huffed.

"You were sure interested in me when you felt me against you."

"I was mistaken."

"Another woman, I'd understand, but for the life of me, I can't figure out why you're with a man." Gi looked around the crowd. "Where is he, by the way?" she asked innocently.

"I don't know," Taren said, frustrated, ignoring the jab. There's no way she'd ever tell Gi the truth. She wasn't the only woman Taren had slept with, but she was definitely the only woman Taren had ever wanted. She was with Ken because it was easy and over the course of their relationship, she'd learned to love him. She knew she'd never have what she had with Gi, that kind of unbridled passion was a once in a lifetime experience, but she was happy where she was. "I never left your side when we went out. If he was smart, he wouldn't either."

Taren scanned the crowd, looking for her beau.

"I'm serious about the offer. We both know you're the best person for the job."

Taren stepped closer. "I'm not getting involved with anything illegal, Gi."

Gi shook her head. "Have I ever lied to you, tesoro?" she asked. "Besides, you've seen the books. You'd know if I was hiding something."

Taren clamped her jaw shut, knowing Gi was right. Lying hadn't been their problem. "Give me a week," she sighed before disappearing into the crowd.

\*\*\*

Ken and their friends were standing at the bar when Taren finally found them.

"Want another drink?" he asked.

"No. I have a headache from the loud music," she answered.

"We can go if you want. This place isn't really my scene either."

Taren nodded, knowing she could've easily stayed all night if she'd been in Gi's arms again.

\*\*\*

Taren thought about the job for the rest of the weekend as she lounged around on the couch. Ken went to play golf with some work friends on Sunday, which gave her the place to herself. The lucrative salary was definitely a factor, but working with Gi again could be disastrous. She was happy with her everyday life. Ken was good to her and she loved him, albeit in a different way than she'd loved Gi. She loved him because he was sweet and kind, and would never do anything to hurt anyone. She wasn't exactly in love with him, but she didn't feel like she needed to be to have a life with him.

If she took this job, she'd most definitely have to keep the past in the past. She was a different person now and Gi would have to see that. Ken knew absolutely nothing about her college years, except that she went to UCLA. She had no idea what he would say if he ever found out she was involved with a woman, much less an illegal gambling ring. She'd have to find a way to keep her past and present from colliding, or she'd lose everything.

***

Ken arrived home late Sunday afternoon. Taren had mentally drained herself thinking about the job offer and its consequences, and had fallen asleep on the couch. Ken ran his hand over her arm softly until she stirred.

"Hey," she said groggily. "I can't believe I fell asleep. What time is it?" She sat up, looking for the nearest clock.

"Almost four," he replied, sitting down next to her. "How was golf?"

"I got my ass kicked as usual, but it was fun. Paul was pretty hungover, so he didn't play as well as he usually does."

Taren laughed softly and placed her head on her shoulder and her hand on his chest as he slipped his arm around her.

"He said they had a great time last night. I told him to let me know the next time they go to a bar because we're definitely not nightclub people."

Taren nodded. "Are you hungry?" she asked.

"Sure. An early dinner sounds good. I need to go shower. Order whatever you want," he replied, kissing the top of her head before getting up.

# *Chapter 8*

When Taren got to work on Wednesday, she found out the firm wasn't giving third quarter bonuses due to their poor second quarter. Plus, all the accounts managers were taking on ten more clients because another senior accountant was retiring and they were not going to replace him. She could barely keep up with the accounts she already had because the guy she replaced hadn't done much of anything with them in the past two years. She was still consulting many of her clients on retirement savings plans and money market shares. Her job as an accountant was to always make sure their books were perfect and find to save them money.

*Of course, Gi gives me an offer that's impossible to refuse and this place goes to hell,* she thought. Taren arrived home just after Ken. He was standing in the bedroom, loosening his tie when she walked in. He'd barely said hello when she began telling him about her day. After a good bout of venting, Ken looked thoughtfully at her.

"Maybe you should start looking, too," he said.

"Actually…" Taren sat on the edge of the bed. "I've already been given an offer."

"Really? Where?"

"My largest client, actually."

"That's great. Are they looking for an in-house accountant?"

"Yes and no." She bit the corner of her mouth. "It's a financial director position," she explained, going on to tell him about the large salary increase.

"Why haven't you said yes? A pay increase and a huge advancement opportunity? Sounds like a great job."

*Because my ex-girlfriend, who used to be a criminal and may currently be working for the mob,owns the company. Oh, and by the way, I used to be her criminal accountant.* Taren rubbed her temples. She contemplated telling him she knew Gi, but decided against it. "I wasn't sure if I could handle the job," she lied.

"Sure you can, hun. I think it's a great opportunity." He smiled and pushed his glasses up before kissing her softly.

"I actually know the owner."

"Oh, really? You mean beyond picking them up as an account?"

"Yeah. We were acquaintances through mutual friends in college. I didn't realize it was her at first. Then, I wanted to make sure she was hiring me because of what I've done with her account and not because we used to know each other."

"That makes sense. What company is it?"

"R&R Enterprises. As in Rapture and Rogue."

"Oh. Wow, so your friend owns all of that?"

"Yes, she built it from the ground up."

"What's her name?

"I doubt you'd know her. Gianna Revisi."

He nodded, stepping closer and kissing her softly. "Doesn't ring a bell. Anyway, I'm happy for you. This is going to be great."

\*\*\*

The next morning, Taren drove to Rapture before heading to her office. She had to ring the bell to get in since the bar wasn't open yet.

"Can I help you?" the woman in the intercom asked.

"Taren Rauley to see Gianna Revisi," Taren replied.

After two minutes of silence, the lock on the door clicked. Taren swung it open and walked around to the elevator. When the doors parted, she nearly ran headfirst into Gi who was exiting.

"I didn't expect you to come down," Taren said.

"If you're here, I'm assuming you've decided to take the job," Gi replied, nodding towards a table. "Either that or you wanted to see me again." She grinned.

"If I do this, Gi, we have to have some ground rules," Taren said, all business.

Gi shrugged.

"I'm not getting back with you. Our past has nothing to do with this."

"If I wanted you back, I'd have you by now." Gi folded her hands together in front of her and locked her blue eyes on Taren's face. "What else?"

"Ken has no knowledge of my college days."

"That doesn't surprise me," Gi murmured, a little hurt.

"I'm serious. He can never know anything about our past together. In fact, no one can."

"Your lesbian indiscretions are safe with me," Gi said, rolling her eyes.

"How did you get out of going to jail when the ring was busted?" Taren changed the subject. The question had been weighing on her mind since she'd first seen Gi at Rapture.

"Oh, you heard about that?"

"It was in the statewide news." Taren crossed her arms, remembering when she read the story about it in the paper.

"Well, you know my family is well connected…"

"Are you serious? The *mob* got you out?"

Gi laughed. "You were always so gullible. I loved that about you the most."

"Get to the point," Taren huffed.

"I wasn't involved anymore. I'd already sold the business to Jackson William."

"You knew the heat was coming and you got out to save your own ass." Taren deduced, remembering Gi's uncanny ability to thwart the authorities. "Typical Gi."

"I sold him a business that was completely off the grid. The cops tried to figure out who was behind everything when I was running the operation, but they never had a chance. I stayed two steps ahead of them."

"Why get out then, if it wasn't because you knew the cops were close? That business was your baby."

Gi pulled her eyes away and stared blankly at the booth a few feet away.

"What made you leave?" Taren urged.

Ice cold blue eyes bore into her as Gi turned her head. "You," she murmured.

"Me?"

"You broke my heart, Taren. I didn't care about anything after that."

Taren felt the coolness of Gi's eyes all the way to her spine. Gi rarely called her Taren.

"I don't believe you," Taren replied. "You'd say anything to make me feel guilty for leaving you."

Gi shrugged. "I'm past the point of caring about why you left or what you did afterwards."

"If there was no heat, why did Jackson get busted?" Taren asked, pushing further.

"He got greedy and started allowing people in off the street that weren't checked out first. He let a wired nark inside and they got him."

"What about your friends? You let them go to jail, too."

"I didn't let anyone do anything, Taren. I told them I was getting out. It's not my fault they stayed!" she growled angrily. "Who gives a shit? It's over now. You moved on to play house with Ken, and I…well, I moved on, too. Those who stayed, it was their choice," she sighed.

"Leave Ken out of this, please."

"You can't possibly be attracted to him." Gi shook her head.

"You have no idea who or what I'm attracted to,"Taren exclaimed. "Anyway, he's off limits."

"Off limits?" Gi raised an eyebrow.

"I'm not going to work here if you're constantly bashing my relationship. My personal life is none of your business. This is a working relationship between you and me, or it's nothing."

Gi sighed and nodded. "Waste your life with that flimsy old goat if you want. I don't care anymore."

Taren pinned her with a glare. Gi shrugged. "You brought up the past, not me."

"I've talked myself in and out of taking this job at least a hundred times. I'm probably making the biggest mistake of my life."

"Then why the hell are you here?"

"I don't know," Taren sighed. "It's a great opportunity and despite our past, I'd be stupid not to take it."

Gi nodded. "Where does this leave us?" She checked her watch.

"I need to give Nicholson my notice, but I can start after that."

"They'll fire you, so you might as well start tomorrow."

"No they won't," Taren retorted.

"Most companies get rid of anyone who has financial access or handles important documents as soon as they give notice. You should know this."

"I doubt they'll let me go."

"Okay, suit yourself. My assistant will set you up with an office, as well as the door code. Give her a call when you're ready to start. I'll give you the computer codes myself." She stood and pushed the chair back in.

"Is that it?" Taren asked.

"Yes. Welcome to the company and all that. I need to get to a meeting." Gi noticed the odd expression on Taren's face. "What? Do you need a hug or something?"

"Hell no," Taren said as she stood up.

They walked out together and Taren was barely in her car when she saw Gi's sports car careen out of the parking lot. She couldn't believe she'd actually taken the job. She prayed that it wasn't a mistake and reminded herself that she was the one who walked away from Gi, not the other way around, although it was starting to feel like it the more she was around her. She wondered if she was going to be able to work alongside Gi effectively and keep the past in the past. She wasn't exactly lying to Ken by not telling him about her past, but she hated adding another barrier between them.

# *Chapter 9*

Taren punched in the door code and waited for the lock to click. She took a deep breath, letting it out slowly as she entered the ground floor of Rapture. No one was downstairs at 7:45 a.m. She was three days into her new job and so far she'd barely seen anyone except the receptionist and occasionally Gi's assistant. She hadn't seen Gi.

"Good morning, Ms. Rauley," the receptionist said when Taren stepped off the elevator.

"Sam, you can call me Taren. I won't bite your head off." Taren smiled.

"Oh, yes she will. Don't let her fool you," Gi teased from a few feet away.

Taren spun around.

"Do you have a minute?" Gi asked.

"Sure. I was wondering when I'd see you," Taren replied, walking with her down the hallway.

"Miss me?" Gi teased.

"No. I've been sitting in limbo for the past two days."

"I should've known you'd want to hit the ground running." Gi opened her office door and nodded for Taren to step inside. "I had some offsite meetings to go to. I told you they'd let you go when you gave notice." She smiled.

Taren didn't comment as she took a seat across from Gi's desk. Gi walked around, sat in the wingback chair and turned on her computer monitors.

"How's your office?" Gi asked while she waited for the system to start.

"Fine."

"What is it?" Gi asked, noticing the questioning look on Taren's face.

"Nothing." Taren stared at the large window behind Gi. "With a company this large, I'm surprised you don't have more employees."

Gi pulled her deep blue eyes from the monitors to look at her. "Trust is not something I come by easily, you know that."

Taren nodded, remembering how the two of them had run the entire gambling operation together, something Gi had previously done alone because she'd trusted no one, until Taren.

"I actually have an operations manager who oversees the inventory, supply orders, and hiring for both bars. You haven't met because he's working on our newest project. He's also fairly new to the company." Gi typed for a moment and the printer began chattering. "Here are your codes. Memorize them and shred this. You are the only person in this company, besides me, who has access to everything." Gi met her eyes with a serious expression.

"You're trusting me with a lot," Taren murmured, taking the printout.

"Trust was never an issue with us," Gi explained. "Anyway, you'll be able to look at each establishment separately, then as a whole, from day one until today."

"Is this a test?" Taren asked, waiting for the other shoe to drop.

"What do you mean?"

"Am I supposed to go through all of your financials to see if I find the illegal side of the business? Or am I simply the guinea pig that's going to unknowingly cover everything up for you?"

"Taren…" Gi sighed. "We've been down this road. My company is legit. I left the illegal activity behind me. I hired you because the company is growing quickly. I need help and I trust you."

Despite her objections, Taren knew Gi had never lied to her, and she didn't see a reason for her to start now. She folded the printout in half and slid it into her briefcase.

Gi watched Taren squeeze her eyes shut, before opening them and pinning her with an unmasked gaze. It was the first time since they'd reconnected that Taren had looked at her with the same naked eyes she'd used when they were together. Gi felt her chest tighten.

"I trust you, Gi," Taren murmured honestly before pulling her eyes away and standing up.

***

Taren spent the rest of the week getting to know the computer system. Gi's company worked on multiple platforms with a high level of security which was both smart and a pain in the ass. Before she left on Friday, Taren created a new spreadsheet format which had the bar and nightclub separated first as two entities, then together as one business. This would make it easier for her to research company records as a whole. She planned to make additional spreadsheets for each year the company had been in business, so she at least had a cheat sheet if something came up that she needed to research.

Taren stepped out of her office, locking the door behind her, when she heard Gi's voice. She turned in the direction of her office and saw the older, mob-looking guy she'd seen a few times walk into Gi's office.

"Hey." Gi smiled, noticing Taren. She shut the door behind him and walked to meet her.

Taren had only seen her once this week, and now the mysterious suited man was back.

"I'm combining information from all of the systems into a set of spreadsheets and cheat sheets for myself. I'm nowhere near finished, so I'll probably be in over the weekend," Taren said.

"Do you need any help?" Gi asked.

"No. I know how you are about assistants. The more eyes on the cookie jar, the more hands touching the cookies," she replied, quoting something Gi had always said about having too many people involved in their affairs.

Gi laughed. "I meant me. Would you like me to come in and help you?"

"Oh." Taren shook her head. "No," she added. "I'll get it done."

"Okay." Gi turned to go back to her office, but paused and spun around. "Hey, do you remember when we went to Cancun?"

Taren wasn't in the mood for a stroll down memory lane, but how could she ever forget the vacation from hell? "Yeah, what about it?"

"I think that was when I really knew…" she trailed off, thinking out loud.

"Knew what?" Taren prompted. Gi snapped out of her nostalgia.

"Nothing. My cousin just got back and he had a similar experience. It made me think of our trip."

\*\*\*

On the drive home, Taren couldn't stop her mind from scrolling through memories of the Cancun trip. She and Gi had only been together a few months and were still growing closer. They had both been so excited, but as soon as they'd arrived, everything went to hell. The A/C in their room barely worked and it smelled like cat pee; the airline lost their luggage until the day they left; their party boat started taking on water and barely made it back to the dock; and they'd both picked up a stomach bug that left them fighting over the bathroom.

Taren shook her head and smiled at the memories of a time when she was head over heels in love and nothing else in the world mattered. "Another lifetime," she whispered to herself as she pulled up to her brownstone.

\*\*\*

Ken was sitting on the couch, dressed in a suit, with a huge smile on his face, and tapping his foot like a kid with a secret. "Hey!" he said excitedly as he jumped up to kiss her. "How was your day?"

"Fine," she replied cautiously. "What's going on?" she asked, never seeing him act like this.

"I made special dinner plans to celebrate your first week, Ms. Financial Director." He smiled.

Taren laughed. "Do I get to know what this surprise is?"

"Nope!" He grinned like a little boy.

Taren went into the bedroom to change from her skirt suit to a knee length, black cocktail dress with deep Vs in the front and back, and a pair of black peep-toe sling-backs.

***

Taren stared out the window, trying to figure out where they were headed as Ken drove them across town towards the river. He finally turned into a lot and waited for the valet. Taren followed him, taking his hand as they walked along the sidewalk at Navy Pier.

"Are we taking a dinner cruise?" she asked.

"Yes," he answered, pointing to the small cruise ship nearby.

"Wow," she exclaimed.

As soon as they boarded, they were shown to the upper deck where large floor-to-ceiling windows surrounded the room. The waiter sat them next to one of the windows. Then he reached for the bottle of champagne that was chilling in a bucket on a stand nearby. Taren watched as he dropped strawberries into each glass, then poured the champagne over top of them. She smiled and lifted the table d'hôte style menu.

She and Ken looked over all of the decadent choices and decided on their meal as the boat pushed off the dock and began motoring down the river.

"This is nice," Taren said, smiling at him.

"To the future," Ken replied, holding up his glass and clinking it against hers.

***

They chose to leave work behind, instead talking about the interesting scenery over dinner. As soon as they'd

63

finished dessert, they walked out onto the deck. Taren gripped the railing and looked up. The dark, cloudless sky had a handful of stars and a full moon shining brightly.

"Thank you," Taren said, cuddling close to Ken and linking her arm through his.

"You're welcome. I wanted to celebrate your promotion, but that's not the only reason we're here," he replied, reaching into his pocket.

Taren's heart leapt into her throat as he bent down on one knee.

"Taren Rauley, you're the best thing that's ever happened to me. I love you with everything I am and I'd like nothing more than to share my life with you. Will you marry me?" He smiled at her as he opened the box, revealing a solitaire, diamond ring on a platinum band.

Taren was in shock. She began nodding her head. "Yes!" she exclaimed.

The small crowd around them cheered as he pushed the ring onto her finger and stood to kiss her. Taren threw her arms around him as he hugged her close.

"I love you," he whispered.

"I love you, too," she replied. She hadn't said the words often, but when she did, she meant them.

# *Chapter 10*

Taren was tired on Monday morning. She and Ken had only had two short lovemaking sessions, but they'd spent the weekend watching movies together and riding all over the city, looking at houses they couldn't afford.

She was sitting at her desk inputting information into her spreadsheets when Gi walked in.

"I thought you were working over the weekend," Gi said, taking a seat across from her.

"I was, but something came up."

Gi nodded. "I want you to sit in on a meeting this Thursday. There are some people you need to meet."

Taren raised a brow, wondering if she was referring to the suited men who kept appearing. "Are they vendors?"

"No, they're all part of this organization. One is the new operations manager and the other two are part of the new endeavor that has been taking up so much of my time."

"What are you talking about?" Taren asked.

"A third establishment. No one knows about it yet, but we've been gutting and remodeling an old building for the past two weeks."

"Okay…" she sighed. "Who is we?"

"I went into business with my uncle and cousins," Gi said.

"As the financial director of this company, when were you going to tell me about this?"

"I'm telling you now, which is why I want you to start sitting in on our meetings."

"Why isn't any of this in the company financial records?"

"It is, which is why you found the discrepancy, but for the most part, it's off the books until we open it."

"Why all the secrecy?"

Gi reached over the desk, pulling Taren's left hand up. "You tell me," she replied, looking at the glistening ring.

"My personal life is off the table," Taren sneered.

Gi dropped her hand and shook her head. "So is mine."

"Why are you bringing me into the meetings?"

"Because the new business is going to be under R&R until it gets established, then I'll cut it loose. So, you'll need to know what's going on financially."

"I'll need access to the accounts before the next meeting."

"You already have it, which is why I'm surprised you haven't come asking about everything, but I see you've been busy."

Taren folded her hands in the middle of her desk, refusing to take the bait.

Gi reached over, placing her hand on Taren's as she stood.

"Are you happy?" Gi asked softly.

Taren tried to pull her eyes away, but she couldn't. Gi walked away before she could answer.

\*\*\*

A week later, Taren turned the corner to enter the elevator and the three suited men were waiting to go up as well. She took a step back, feeling uncomfortable around Gi's mobster family members. The youngest one, who looked like Gi, grinned at her as his eyes ran down her body. She made sure her engagement ring glistened as she moved her left hand to her face.

When the doors opened, the oldest man stepped aside and waved for her to enter. "Beautiful ladies first," he said with a smile.

Taren forced a smile and walked to the back of the elevator. "Thank you," she murmured as they stepped inside.

The doors closed and parted once again at the next floor. The men strolled out, followed by Taren.

"Ms. Revisi is expecting you," the receptionist said.

The youngest one turned around and offered his hand.

"I'm Mario," he stated with a big grin.

"Taren," she replied, shaking his hand.

"Mario, *muovilo!*" the older man barked, shaking his head.

"I hope to see you again soon," the young man said, before hustling to catch up with the other two.

Taren rolled her eyes as she walked over to her desk. She'd barely sat down when her phone rang.

"Taren Rauley," she answered, wondering who was calling her before eight in the morning.

"Did you forget the meeting?" Gi asked on the other end.

"No. I thought the meeting was at eight. I just got here."

"You know Italians are always early and two steps ahead. Didn't you wonder who those guys in the elevator were?"

"I figured those were your family members, but they look like the mob," Taren answered.

Gi laughed and hung up.

\*\*\*

When Taren walked into Gi's office, she noticed Gi and the older man were sitting in the chairs and the two younger men were on the couch. A large blueprint was laid out on the coffee table.

"This is Taren Rauley, my new Financial Director," Gi said as she stood and waved her into the room. "Taren, this is my uncle, Bruno Revisi," she added, pointing to the older man. "And these are my cousins, Sergio and Mario."

"We've met," Mario said with a wink in Taren's direction.

Gi raised a questioning eyebrow, and Taren simply shrugged as she sat down next to him.

"Mario is the new Operations Manager I told you about."

Sergio stuck out his hand and introduced himself.

"I'm sorry it's taken so long for me to get everyone on the same page," Gi stated. "This is Gentlemen's Rook," she spread her hands over the blueprints. "It's going to be a bi-level cigar bar and whiskey lounge when it's finished."

"Wow," Taren said.

"Not what you were expecting?" Gi asked.

"I never really know what to expect with you," she laughed.

"Sounds like she knows you well," Bruno said.

"Something like that," Gi answered. "Anyway, I have everyone together today because we're less than two months away from opening the doors to GR. I'm getting the licensing taken care of this week. Taren will need to know every product that moves in and out from this point forward, as everything will be under R&R Enterprises. She needs to a part of the approval process for everything from here on." She paused. "Taren, Sergio will be the manager of the new bar."

"I am happy to meet you and look forward to working with you," Bruno said, holding his hand out to Taren, which she shook.

"Thanks. It's nice to meet members of Gi's family." *Finally,* she thought.

"Oh, that's a pretty rock. You must have a lucky man on your arm." Bruno grinned, noticing the diamond glistening on her other hand.

Taren smiled graciously.

"All right," Gi stated, changing the subject. "Over the next three weeks, we'll be finishing the renovations; plus stocking the humidor and the bar, and hiring staff. Uncle Bruno has been working with various agencies to get highly talented wait staff and Sergio has already lined up the best vendors to stock everything. We're waiting for the interior to be finished so we can get the place inspected and ready to go in time. The ad will start running two weeks prior to the opening. The next three weeks are going to be pretty crazy."

"Sounds like a plan," Bruno agreed.

"Mario, make sure you get all of the vendor information to Taren by the end of the day. She'll need to have them in the system so she can balance the supply invoices."

"No problem," he replied.

"Sergio, don't forget you're meeting with tile guy this afternoon. Check our sample against his and make sure he has the correct batch this time," Bruno scolded. "That fuckhead showed up with the wrong one yesterday and tried to install it."

"Yes, sir."

"If that's it, I'll check in with you guys later," Gi said, standing and hugging each of her family members.

Sergio and Bruno shook Taren's hand and Mario hung back, giving her the once over again and smiling as he also shook her hand.

Gi watched the interaction, smiling when Taren looked at her and rolled her eyes. As soon as the guys were gone, Gi closed the door and turned back to Taren, who was standing nearby.

"Were those the mobsters you kept accusing me of laundering money with?"

Taren bit her lower lip. "They look like the mob, with their expensive suits and gelled hair."

Gi laughed. "Come here," she said, walking over to where the old photos hung above the couch. "This is the real mob." She pointed. "That's my great-grandfather, Giancarlo Revisi with Al Capone during prohibition."

"Are you serious?" She stepped closer, easily recognizing the famous mobster in the photo. "I guess that's where you get your name from." Taren said.

"Yep," Gi replied. "This one here is my grandfather, Vinny Revisi and Sam Giancana in the late 1950s. The little boy with them is my dad, Franco."

Taren looked closely at all the different pictures. "I know you said your family was connected to the mob, but I figured that was something all Italians said."

"No," Gi laughed. "It's very real."

"So, what about now? Is your family still connected?"

"Oh, no. My grandfather died of a heart attack when my father was a teenager and my father never wanted anything to do with the Outfit as he got older." She stepped away from the couch. "Uncle Bruno and my cousins will be the first to tell you all about the Revisi mob connection. They still act like mobsters," she laughed.

"What is your father doing these days?" Taren asked. "I remember him visiting and taking us to dinner."

Gi sighed. "He always liked you," she said with a thin smile. "He was diagnosed with cancer when I was living in Paris, about a year after you left. I came home to spend time with him. He died about two months later."

"Oh, Gi...I'm so sorry," Taren stepped forward, wrapping her arms around the taller woman without thinking about it.

Gi wrapped her arms around Taren's waist, reveling in the closeness. The feeling of Gi's body against hers sent a familiar shiver down Taren's spine. She closed her eyes, slowly breathing in the essence of the woman in her arms until she realized where she was and who she was with and pulled away.

Taren looked up at the questioning blue eyes staring at her. Unable to speak, she simply put her hand softly on Gi's cheek and walked away.

# *Chapter 11*

The following week, Taren walked towards her car in the side parking lot, when a dark sports car rolled to a stop in front of her. She stood with her hand on her hip. Gi's smiling face appeared when the dark window was lowered.

"Where are you headed?" Gi asked casually.

"Lunch."

"Me, too. Hop in."

Taren raised an eyebrow. "What makes you think I want to go to lunch with you?"

"Because I'm buying. Besides, I want to show you something." Gi said. "Unless you have a lunch date with your old man?"

"Not funny and no," Taren muttered, shaking her head as she made her way to the passenger side. "I thought you were a BMW person," she said, buckling her seatbelt.

The luxury car had black leather interior with carbon fiber and brushed aluminum trim. Taren barely got a look before Gi put it in gear and drove away.

"I guess my tastes have changed over the years," Gi replied without looking over.

"Uh huh," Taren murmured. "I see you're still into Pink," she laughed, nodding her head to the faint music playing on the sound system.

"Some things will never change," Gi added, finally looking her way.

A few minutes later, they pulled into the parking lot of a popular restaurant. "You still eat sushi, don't you?" Gi asked with a hint of playful sarcasm.

Taren ignored the jab as she got out and walked inside without looking at her. They were shown to a two-person table in the back of the small establishment.

\*\*\*

They spent the next half hour eating and sharing an array of sushi rolls. Taren managed to keep R&R their main topic. The bill arrived, and Gi changed to subject.

"Do you remember that hole-in-the-wall place we used to go to in L.A.?" Gi asked, placing her bank card in the billfold.

"Yeah," Taren laughed. "I used to think that had the best food, but this was excellent."

"Yeah, I come here a lot."

Taren nodded. "I can't remember the last time I ate sushi, actually."

"Seriously? It's your favorite food."

"Ken doesn't like it."

Gi rolled her eyes and smirked, wanting to say something else. She shook her head instead. She had a hard time believing this reserved and passive person was the same tenacious and unrestricted Taren who got what she wanted, always on her own terms.

"Thank you for lunch," Taren said.

"Sure. I'm calling it a business meeting anyway, so you'll get the bill," Gi replied, signing the slip.

"You said you wanted to show me something," Taren stated when they stepped outside.

"We're going by the new place," Gi replied, removing her sunglasses and sliding them into the inside pocket of her suit jacket once she was behind the darkly tinted glass of the car windows.

Taren checked her email on her phone as they drove down the road. When they came to a stop in another parking lot she glanced around, looking for the new bar, but they were sitting in the parking lot of a rundown shopping center.

"Where are we?" Taren asked, stowing her phone in her purse.

"We have a little time to kill," Gi replied. "Do you still eat cannoli?"

"Not much anymore."

"Let me guess, Ken doesn't like sweets."

"He eats cheesecake like it's going out of style," Taren said.

"Yuck," Gi grimaced. "Come on. This bakery has the best cannoli in town. I've been coming here since I was a kid."

Taren nodded and followed her into the small place. A bell over the door rang loudly and a little, old Italian lady came out, wiping the flour from her hands.

"Gianna Revisi, *dove sei stato nascosto, giovane donna?* Where have you been hiding, young woman?" she said sternly. She then ran around the counter to give Gi a big hug, careful not to get her dark suit covered in pastry flour.

"*Qui e là, ma soprattutto dietro una scrivania.* Here and there, but mostly behind a desk," Gi replied, She turned to Taren. "This is Carlotta Fiore. She knew my grandparents well."

"Nice to meet you," Taren said with a smile.

"This one treats you good, yes?" Carlotta beamed and pointed to Gi.

Taren laughed and nodded.

"What can I get for you both?"

"Two cannoli," Gi answered.

The older woman removed two fresh pastries from behind the counter, set them on a plate, and handed it to Gi. Taren followed her over to a bistro-style table.

"Oh, my God, this is good!" Taren exclaimed, chewing her first bite. Eating the Italian dessert brought back a lot of memories for Taren, which was why she rarely ate it anymore.

"Best in town," Gi replied with a mouth full of food.

"Do you remember the time I tried to make these for your birthday?" Taren snickered.

"Yeah," Gi laughed. "They were horrible!"

"You still ate one!" Taren giggled.

Gi looked in her eyes. "Because you made it for me," she replied.

Taren smiled softly and finished the dessert.

"It's on the house," Carlotta replied when they stepped over to pay.

"You don't have to do that," Gi argued, knowing she'd already lost this battle.

Carlotta winked at her and said, "*Mi ricordo di essere in amore*."

Gi hugged her again.

"Thank you," Taren added. As they walked out, she said "That was nice of her."

"She thinks we're in love."

Taren smacked the side of her head on the top of the car, forgetting to duck as she slid into the seat. "Son of a bitch!" she yelped.

"Are you okay?" Gi asked, trying not to laugh.

"Yes," Taren growled, rubbing the side of her head. "What made her think that?"

Gi shrugged. "I've never brought anyone here with me, so she must have assumed I'd finally settled down. Who knows? I haven't seen her in six months, maybe longer."

\*\*\*

When they arrived at the new bar's location, Gi parked, away from the construction trucks.

"Are you sure your head is okay?" she asked, getting out of the car and putting her sunglasses on.

"I'm fine," Taren answered. "How old is this building?"

"It was built in the 1980s, but the idea behind Gentleman's Rook is an old speakeasy. We completely refaced the outside to match the period décor on the inside." Taren walked in.

"Wow," Taren said, impressed. The bar still had a month before the grand opening, but it was coming along nicely. "This is nothing like your other two places."

"This is all Uncle Bruno. I'm funding the operation until it takes off, then I'll hand it over to him."

"I still can't believe you are in business with your family. You always told me you didn't trust anyone enough to have a business partner," Taren said.

Gi shrugged and sighed, "I guess I've changed, too."

"What do you think, huh?" Bruno said, walking up to them. He smiled at Taren and hugged his niece.

"It's impressive." Taren replied.

"Come, let me show you around." He held his arm out.

As soon as they'd walked away, Gi went in search of Sergio.

"What's going on with the fire permit?" she asked, finding him in the back room.

"Hey," Sergio said. "I don't know. The marshal was here a few days ago and said we need to add more sprinklers or upgrade the entire system."

"Are you kidding me?" Gi shook her head. She'd built Rapture and Rogue from the ground up, so she'd never run into the issues that come with bringing an old building up to code. "It's too late to put in a new system. Call the company that worked on the insulation and see if they know someone. Did the marshal say how many more we need?"

"He wrote it down," Sergio explained, walking towards the manager's office. "Here," he said, handing her the pink review sheet.

Gi read the marshal's notes. "He's looking for a minimum of five new units or a replacement system that has at least fifty units. How many units do we have now?"

"Sixty-five."

"Why the hell do we need a newer unit with fewer sprinkler heads? That makes no damn sense."

"The upgraded unit has more pressure, so the heads spray further."

Gi shook her head. "When you get someone in here, ask how much work is involved in upgrading, but keeping the heads we have now and adding ten heads. Let me know what you find out." She started to walk away and turned back to the men. "Has the electrician finished?"

"Yes. All we have left is the sprinkler situation and then we can start getting the fixtures brought in. The guy doing the woodwork on the bar is almost finished. It should be done by the end of the week."

"Did Mario get the supply order in to the vendors?"

"I'm not sure. I know he was working on it."

"Is he still here?"

"I think he was headed over to Rogue," Sergio replied.

Gi nodded and walked away. She was about to call Mario when she heard Taren's laughter nearby. She moved further into the room and found her laughing with Mario standing close, a huge smile plastered to his face and his hand on her shoulder as he told her the punchline of his joke. Gi's teeth ground together.

"Mario," she called. He spun around and lifted his chin in her direction. Gi wanted to smack the smug look off his face as she walked over to him.

"Is the restroom working?" Taren asked.

"Yes, down the hallway," Mario pointed.

"I suggest you find somewhere else to be, like getting the supply orders taken care of," Gi growled.

"What if she wants me here?" he replied with a cocky grin.

"She doesn't and I damn sure don't. You have work to do."

"She's into men, you know."

"I don't give a fuck if she's into bestiality. She's not into you, and if you know what's good for you, you won't be into her," she snapped. "Get that damn supply order finished by the end of the day. Some of the vendors need more than a week for delivery, especially with the cigars."

Taren stepped out from the bathroom hall just as Gi was turning to walk away. Her long, wavy curls fell over one shoulder. The tanned skin of her arms contrasted against the three-quarter sleeves of her bright, white blouse.

"Is everything okay?" Taren asked, pushing her sleeves up. She thought she must've missed something, seeing the anger soften in Gi's eyes.

"Fine." Gi forced a smile. "Are you ready?"

"Sure." Taren answered.

\*\*\*

On her drive home, Taren kept playing the day over in her head. Her animosity towards Gi was starting to wither, and if she was honest with herself, she had no reason to be mad at her. She'd left because the crime business was growing larger and larger and despite her efforts to get Gi to slow down and give it up, Gi kept allowing the expansion and reveled in the power it had given her. Taren could no longer stand by her and watch it destroy Gi's life and potentially her own in the process. Spending the day laughing and talking with Gi reminded her of the happy times in their past.

Taren pulled over, stopping in a small parking lot. She squeezed the top of the steering wheel and sighed as her forehead came to rest against her hands. Feeling a sharp poke, she quickly pulled her head away, revealing the diamond engagement ring. Shaking her head, Taren took that as a sign that her life was different now. She'd rarely thought about Gi, until she'd run into her at Rapture. The

walls she'd worked so hard to build, that blocked that part
of life, were coming down, brick by brick.

# Chapter 12

A few days later, Taren was sitting at her desk, inputting the monthly statements into her spreadsheet so they could be balanced and paid, when she heard a soft knock and her office door swung open. She stopped typing and watched Gi take a seat across from her.

"Hi," Taren said.

"Did Mario send you the vendor list and supply order for GR?"

"No." Taren answered. "I haven't seen any emails and he didn't put it in my inbox."

"Damn it!" she growled.

"What's wrong?" Taren asked.

"He's a pain in my ass! That's what's wrong." Gi huffed. "He's book smart, but completely dumb when it comes to everything clsc," shc sighed. "He needs to get that order in or the bar will open with no supplies. I told him to get it done by the end of the day and send everything to you. That was three days ago."

"I haven't seen it." Taren looked through a stack of papers sitting on the corner of her desk. "Maybe he has it finished but hasn't dropped it off."

"I don't have time to chase him all over town. I have a flight to catch." Gi rubbed her left temple. "I won't be available tomorrow or this weekend and he knows it. Do me a favor and call him in the morning. If you still haven't seen it, I'll do it myself when I return Monday, while he's digging my shoe out of his ass."

Taren nodded and watched Gi leave the room. She was surprised the owner of the company was taking a long weekend when they were knee-deep trying to get the new business running. It finally dawned on her when she glanced at the calendar on her desk. Saturday was the fifteenth, Gi's birthday. Taren jumped up from her desk and headed down the hall to catch her, but the receptionist said she'd already gone downstairs.

As soon as the elevator came to a stop, Taren hurried towards the front door to wish her a happy birthday before she left, but a tall blonde in a short, black mini-dress was standing beside Gi's car. Taren watched as Gi opened the passenger door for her.

\*\*\*

The weekend went by extremely slowly for Taren. She cleaned the apartment, did the laundry, and even went to an art convention with Ken, but nothing made the time pass any faster.

"Something's bothering you," Ken finally said on Sunday evening. "What is it?"

"I'm fine," she sighed. "That time of the month is coming. You know I get irritable and work is driving me crazy."

"I thought things were going great?"

"They are. I guess I'm just stressed because I'm not finished closing out the quarter and the month is half over."

"Are you still busy with the new place?"

"Yeah. That's part of the problem. Spending is all over the place, so the ledger isn't balancing."

"I'm sure you'll get it straightened out." He smiled, wrapping his arm around her. "Did you give any more thought to planning a trip home?"

"Yeah, actually. I was thinking of waiting until after the bar opens, when things slow down."

"Okay, so a month?"

"Something like that."

"Good. I'll take a look at the calendar tomorrow and call you so we can try to put the dates together. I know I have merger meetings coming up, so I don't want to mess up and tell you the wrong dates."

Taren nodded. Going home to San Diego was sounding better and better. She missed her family, and she needed change of scenery more than anything.

\*\*\*

On Monday morning, Taren was walking down the hallway in the office towards the break room, when she heard Gi's voice. She poured herself a cup of coffee and hurried out of the room, trying to avoid Gi, but it was too late. They nearly bumped into each other in the doorway.

"Whoa!" Gi said. "In a hurry, tesoro?" She smiled.

"Something like that," Taren answered, squeezing past her.

"I just got off the phone with Mario." Gi stepped closer. "He said you scared him on the phone."

"Well, you left, so I made sure he got those orders placed," Taren stated.

"Your ferocious side never intimidated me, but it definitely did a lot of other things," Gi teased.

Taren shrugged.

"How was your weekend?" Gi asked, changing the subject.

"Great, as I'm sure yours was, too. I don't have time to hear all about it, so…" Taren turned to walk away.

"What's wrong?" Gi questioned, following her into her office.

"Happy birthday," Taren sneered, standing behind her desk.

"Thanks…I wasn't sure you remembered." Gi leaned her hip against Taren's desk.

Taren set her cup of hot coffee, resisting the urge to throw it at her boss. "Yes…I remembered." She shook her head. "I'm here busting my ass to get the ledger together for the quarter, and with the new business so far off the page, I can't even find half of the shit I'm trying to balance. All the while, you decide to take an impromptu vacation, leaving me to make sure the supplies get ordered for the new bar!" she spat. "So, yeah, I remembered your birthday. I even rushed out to tell you, just in time to see you driving off with your latest conquest."

Gi crossed her arms and raised an eyebrow. "Let me get this straight. You're mad at me because you had to do your job while I took my mother out of town to see an old friend who was sick, and had lunch with the mayor's assistant to talk about campaign donations?"

Taren swallowed the lump in her throat and felt it hit the bottom of her stomach.

"What's really going on here, Taren?" Gi fixed her with a stare. "You can't walk around with that rock on your hand, pretending to be in love with some man, and think you have a right to say anything about who I see or what I do. You gave up that privilege a long time ago."

"You're right," Taren sighed. "I don't know if I can do this."

"Do what?"

"Work here."

"Are you quitting?" Gi snapped.

Taren clenched her jaw. "I don't know...I can't function." She shook her head. "You drive me—"

Taren's cell phone rang on the desk, cutting her off. When her mother's picture appeared she stiffened. Her mother never called her during the day.

"Hello? Mom?"

"Taren, Grammy fell and hit her head last night. She has a bad bruise on her brain that is bleeding and swelling. It doesn't look good, honey. They induced a coma. We won't know anything until they finish the tests."

"Oh, my God, Mom," Taren began to cry. "We'll be on the first flight out. Please tell her I love her."

"I will. Your dad will get you guys from the airport; just let him know when your flight gets in."

Hearing the conversation, Gi wrapped her arms around Taren as soon as she ended the call, and Taren broke down, sobbing on her shoulder like a child while Gi held her.

"I'm so sorry," Gi whispered, kissing the side of Taren's head.

Taren melded into the warm body against her. Deep blue eyes held her gaze.

"You should get your flight booked," Gi murmured, pulling away.

Taren cleared her throat and stepped back. "I..."

"Take all the time you need. I'll handle things while you're gone."

Taren nodded and sat down to book a flight to San Diego, realizing she needed to call Ken. Hands shaking, she picked up the phone.

# *Chapter 13*

Taren spent two days at the hospital with her family. When they finally got word that the medication was reducing the swelling and the bleeding had stopped, the family went to Taren's grandparents' house to eat some of the food people had dropped off for them.

Taren was exhausted from lack of sleep and she'd barely eaten anything except coffee, so when they got the good news, she was as eager as everyone else to go eat and get some sleep.

"There's my girl," her father said when she walked into the living room next to where he and Ken were sitting on the couch talking. "Make sure you thank your boss for that beautiful arrangement," he added, referring to the expensive flower bouquet that had arrived that morning.

"I will," Taren replied.

"Speaking of, how's the new job going?"

"It's good. Gi is expanding to a third establishment, so it's hectic right now, especially with the close of the quarter."

"Gi? As in Gianna Revisi?" Taren's cousin Melanie asked from the doorway.

"Yeah. That's her new boss," Ken replied. "They actually knew each other in college. Didn't you go to UCLA, too?"

"Yep," Melanie replied.

"Did you know her as well?" he asked.

Taren was standing beside him with a serious expression on her face. She met Melanie's eyes and shook her head. Melanie was her best friend in college. She knew all about the gambling ring, which she was completely against. She'd also been the shoulder Taren had cried on when the relationship had ended. She'd always blamed Gi for getting Taren into that mess to begin with.

Melanie shrugged. "Everyone knew Gi, she was quite popular."

"I haven't met her yet. Maybe at the company Christmas party." He smiled, looking up at Taren, who smiled in return, before walking away to take a deep breath. She'd barely made it down the hallway before she was shoved into the guest bedroom.

"What the fuck are you doing with her?" Melanie asked with her arms crossed like a mother scolding a child.

"It's not what you think," Taren replied. "I had no idea she owned R&R or was even in Chicago for that matter."

"So you don't take the damn job, or you quit," Melanie growled, shaking her head. "I thought when I saw you we'd be talking about wedding planning, not Gianna Revisi!"

Taren shrugged, unsure what to say. She knew her cousin was right.

"Are you sleeping with her?"

"No," Taren huffed.

"Do you want to?"

"No!" Taren exclaimed, running her hand through her hair and pushing the long, wavy locks back. "I don't know," she sighed. "I never thought she'd be in my life again, and she's running a legitimate business. You know I wouldn't be working there if she wasn't."

"Legit or not, it still doesn't change the fact that you're working right beside her again." Melanie shook her head.

"Mel, I love Ken."

"Then why the hell are you anywhere near Gianna Revisi? Ask yourself that question."

"I do…I have."

"And?" Melanie asked.

"That's just it. I don't know."

\*\*\*

Two days later, Taren's grandmother's medication was reduced and she woke up. The doctors were still watching her closely, but she was sitting up and talking to her family members by the end of the day.

Feeling better about the situation, Taren and Ken decided head back to Chicago over the weekend, with the promise to return immediately if anything happened. They said their goodbyes to her mother, as well as her aunt and uncle.

Melanie pulled Taren aside just before they left for the airport.

"I love you, you know," Melanie sighed.

"I know. I love you, too." Taren hugged her.

"I only want what's best for you. I want you to be happy."

"You sound like my mother," Taren laughed.

"Well, I am older than you." Melanie smiled.

"By a whopping six months!"

They laughed together.

Ken stepped closer and grabbed Taren's suitcase. "We need to hurry to beat the long security lines," he said with a smile.

"He's too damn sweet," Melanie giggled. "And he's a good catch," she added.

\*\*\*

Taren stared out the plane window. She'd tried reading a magazine, a book, and watching a movie, but she was unable to focus on anything.

"I know you're worried," Ken said, holding her hand. "She looked good and the doctors gave her a good chance of a full recovery."

Taren nodded. Her mind was moving faster than the airplane and her grandmother wasn't the driving force. Gi was on her mind and had been since her conversation with Melanie. She'd questioned her true motive for taking the job a number of times and Melanie had simply brought it to the surface.

Working at R&R alongside Gi was already becoming an issue. Taren had bitten her head off about something that wasn't even her business to begin with. Two months earlier, she was happy with her life and with Ken, but the more time she spent with Gi…the more she missed her.

# Chapter 14

Monday morning, Taren walked into Rapture and headed straight for Gi's office. She was on the phone, so Taren closed the door and leaned against it.

"I'm going to have to call you back, Uncle Bruno," Gi said, hanging up the phone as she stood. "I wasn't expecting you back already," she murmured, moving across the room. "How's your grandmother?"

"Fine," Taren replied, swallowing the lump in her throat. "The flowers were beautiful, thank you."

"It was the least I could do." Gi stopped a couple of feet away. "I know I should've told you what was going on, instead of just leaving you to handle things. I'm sorry," she sighed. "Don't quit. You're a—"

"I'm not here to quit." Taren stepped forward, wrapping her arms around Gi's neck.

"Taren…" Gi whispered, just before their lips came together in a frantic, heated kiss that left both of them breathless.

Taren locked eyes with Gi as she ran her hands over Gi's shoulders, down her chest to her breasts, caressing them in each hand, before moving them back up and leaning in for another tantalizing kiss.

Gi turned, keeping Taren in her arms and their lips locked, Gi backed her up against the door. She reached down with one hand, turning the lock on the knob before grabbing Taren's tight ass. Taren moaned against her mouth and Gi tore her lips away, moving them across her jaw and down her neck, to the opening of her button-down blouse. She reached around with her other hand, opening the buttons one at a time as her mouth traced kisses lower, over the satin bra covering Taren's breasts to the expanse of skin exposed around her navel. Her hand continued to travel, opening the button and zipper of Taren's slacks, revealing the tattoo on her hip bone.

Gi looked up at the eyes watching her. She opened her mouth to say something, but Taren put her finger over Gi's lips and pushed her head down. Gi pulled her pants and thong down, then spread her thighs and buried mouth in the glistening folds. Taren slammed her head back against the door at the first touch of Gi's tongue.

"Easy, tesoro," Gi whispered, licking in slow, steady circles.

Taren's legs trembled, nearly unable to hold her up. Gi pinned her hips firmly against the door and drove her tongue deep inside. Taren moaned loudly, writhing against the cool, metal door. Gi smiled, knowing her old lover. She pulled her tongue out, finishing her off in a steady rhythm of long, hard strokes.

Taren reached down, grabbing Gi's head and holding her right where she wanted her, before releasing a guttural sound as she came.

Gi gave her a second, then stood up, pulling Taren's clothes up with her. Taren wrapped her arms around Gi's neck, kissing her tenderly and tasting herself. Gi rocked her hips against Taren's as she deepened the kiss.

Taren's hand ran down the front of Gi's pantsuit slowly, coming to rest on the waistband of her pants. She was about to open the button when a loud knock at the door brought them crashing back to the present.

"Damn it," Taren whispered, trying to redress quickly.

Gi straightened her clothing and pulled the door open.

"I was walking by and heard a weird noise, like a screeching animal or something. Are you okay?" Gi's assistant asked.

Gi bit back a laugh when she heard Taren gasp. "I'm fine. I bumped my knee on the desk and it hurt like hell. That's probably what you heard."

"Okay." She moved to walk away and turned back. "Have you seen Ms. Rauley? I swore she walked by me this morning."

Gi shook her head. "What did you need her for?"

"Mr. Revisi faxed over the work order and it's cash on delivery so I wanted to make sure she got it."

"COD? What?" Gi grabbed the paper. "Damn it, Sergio!" she snapped. "I'll take care of it," she told her assistant.

Gi closed the door and immediately went for her cell phone, almost forgetting about the disheveled woman standing a few feet away.

"What did he do?" Taren asked.

"He paid the contractor for the sprinkler system COD, and it was four grand!"

"What?" Taren glanced at the invoice. "This doesn't sound right."

"I know." Gi focused on her and smiled softly. "I need to go over there, but…"

"Look, Gi…I don't even know…what this is," Taren stammered, waving her hand back and forth between them. It had all happened so quickly. She needed time to digest it.

Gi nodded and headed towards the door.

"What the hell have you done?" Taren whispered to herself. She waited a few minutes, then walked to the bathroom.

Taren stared at herself in the mirror and shook her head. "It was a one-time thing," she whispered, knowing she'd gone after what she wanted without even thinking about it. Gi had been on her mind so much lately that she hoped this was what she needed to get the enticing woman out of her head. She'd done it and it was over, so she no longer had to dream about it.

# *Chapter 15*

Taren was happy to see Gi's car wasn't in the lot when she arrived at work. She'd spent most of the night trying to forget about what had transpired less than twenty-four hours ago. She barely ate and didn't sleep. The haunting images of Gi's face buried between her legs rolled like a projection screen behind her closed eyes.

"Damn it," she whispered, chucking an ink pen across the room. She stood up and moved to pick it as her office door opened.

"I thought I heard you come in," Gi said.

"You mean you saw me on the monitor," Taren corrected, moving to put the pen on her desk, distancing herself from Gi. "I didn't think you were here. Your car's not outside."

"My Audi's getting serviced, so I'm in a rental."

Taren nodded.

"And I didn't see you on the monitor. I heard you talking in the hallway."

Taren nodded again, then ran a hand through her hair, pushing it over her shoulder. "Look, Gi…I…" she sighed. "I made a huge mistake."

Gi shrugged. She didn't believe her, but it's what she'd expected.

"It can't happen again." Taren crossed her arms. "It won't happen again."

"Great," Gi said matter-of-factly. "I actually came in to tell you to go ahead and input that invoice from the sprinkler company."

Taren raised an eyebrow.

"I paid the guy yesterday, so he could get started."

"I need the check number," Taren said.

"It was cash."

"Okay, what account did it come out of?" Taren made a note on a piece of paper lying on her desk.

"My pocket," Gi answered.

Taren locked eyes with her. "Who carries four-thousand dollars in their pocket, Gi?"

"I don't normally do that, but I happened to have it on me at the time to put it in the downstairs safe for the tills, so I paid him. There's no need to do anything with the transaction. Make a note that I paid him on the side or something. I just don't want him getting paid twice. Sergio already let him fuck us over with his price to begin with," Gi said.

"All right," Taren replied, changing the wording on her desk note, before facing her again. "Are we good then?"

Gi looked into her eyes and grinned. "Yeah," she murmured.

Taren watched her walk out of the room, wondering how in the hell she was ever going to forget what they'd done.

\*\*\*

Taren saw Gi here and there during the rest of the week, but mostly tried to avoid her. She was happy to see the weekend arrive as she walked out of her closet, dressed in a plain cocktail dress and black heels. Ken turned around and smiled as he tied his tie.

"Thank you for going to this dinner with me," he said.

"Sure." She smiled.

"You'll like my boss and his wife," he added, slipping into his jacket. "You look pretty, by the way."

"Thanks." She smiled.

"Are we ready?"

Taren nodded. She actually had no desire whatsoever to go to dinner with Ken's boss and his wife, but she couldn't simply say no.

*\*\*\**

The food at the five-star restaurant was either seriously lacking flavor or Taren was so far away from herself that she couldn't taste it. The company at the table hadn't helped matters. Ken's boss was stuck on himself and his wife was more like a puppet on a string. No matter how hard she tried, Taren couldn't get Gi off her mind. The more alcohol she drank, the more she swore she could feel Gi's presence.

Ken and his boss were oblivious as they talked business and nursed cocktails like a pair of nerdy old friends. The boss's wife was in her own world with a steady flow of Cosmopolitans coming from the bar. Taren wondered if this was the life she was destined to live: the sidekick wife who kept the bar tab open while her husband stroked his nerd ego with his friends. She cared for him so much, but when he started talking about infrastructure and conglomeration, he was like a windup toy with an inflatable head. Most of the time, she let him get it all out while she nodded and sang her favorite tune in her head. What they had worked, or at least it had for the last year and a half.

\*\*\*

Later that night, as Ken moved closer, kissing her softly, she imagined Gi's mouth on hers; Gi's hands caressing her skin; Gi moving against her as she urged the kiss deeper, inticing a heated connection. Minutes later, the prick of Ken's penis brought her back to reality as he rolled on top of her.

"Is it okay?" Ken asked, noticing a difference in her.

"Yeah. The drinks gave me a headache," she lied.

He moved off of her. "We don't have to do anything tonight," he replied.

She felt bad knowing she'd started it and left him hard and ready, so she reached down, giving him relief with her hand.

As she rolled over to go to sleep, Taren wondered why she was able to have sex with Ken the night before, yet tonight, thoughts of Gi had driven her to forget who she was with. She'd never once thought of someone else while being intimate with Ken, and it made her angry and nervous knowing Gi had that power.

"Are you alright?" Ken questioned, rubbing her back when he felt her sit up.

"Yeah. I'm going to take some Advil and get some air. Go back to sleep," she replied, twisting and kissing him softly.

Taren walked through the living room and stepped onto the balcony. The city lights glowed in the darkened sky. A few stars and a quarter moon were visible in the distance. She sat in the lounge chair and kicked her feet up.

*Get it together,* she thought. As much as she'd wanted to leave Gi in the past, she couldn't. As much as she'd wanted to forget about their encounter, she couldn't. Gianna Revisi was very much in the present. Taren wasn't sure who she was angrier with: herself for completely losing control or Gi for responding so eagerly. Life with Ken was easy, safe, and predictable, but in a good way. On the other hand, life was Gi was always spontaneous, passionate, and somewhat dangerous.

# *Chapter 16*

The following Monday, Taren walked into the break room and Gi appeared in front of her. Taren tried to avoid the questioning blue eyes and sly grin that had haunted her dreams all weekend.

"Are you ignoring me now?" Gi asked.

"Out of sight, out of mind," Taren replied, reaching for the coffee pot.

Gi stepped closer.

"I'm not doing this, Gi," Taren murmured.

"Not doing what?"

"Damn you." Taren shook her head. "It should've never happened. Why did you let it?"

"I'm not the one who's taken," Gi shot back.

Taren clinched her fist as her pulse began to race. "Leave my personal life out of this."

"Okay, nothing personal...got it. So, this thing between us...it's purely physical then," Gi nodded. "Fine with me."

"That is more your style, isn't it?" Taren spat, desire burning in her eyes.

"Don't start something you can't finish," Gi whispered, moving a little closer.

"Damn you. I'm not doing this," Taren growled. She wanted desperately to make her life with Ken go back to the way it was before Gi had appeared. Everything was controlled and in order. Gi had turned her world upside-down, causing her to question everything and crave that fiery passion she knew was just below Gi's surface. "Damn you," she said again, this time mostly directed at herself for getting so caught up in her own inner turmoil.

"You used to take what you wanted, when, where, and how didn't matter. What happened to that girl?" Gi whispered. "You're nothing but a shell of the person you used to be, hiding behind some fake persona because you're scared to be yourself."

"Fuck you, Gi," Taren spat.

Gi moved again, leaving very little space between them. "Oh, you want to. I can see it in your eyes," she whispered, inches from her lips.

Taren lost it as she reached up, forcefully pulling Gi into a kiss. Their bodies slammed together as their mouths fought for control. Taren ran her hands down, squeezing Gi's breasts and moving further, around to her ass. Gi kissed her hard, biting her lip as her hand ran lower, cupping Taren's sex and feeling the wetness through her dark slacks.

Taren moaned into her mouth and Gi pulled away, putting a few inches between them. Taren raised an eyebrow as Gi turned towards the door.

"I hate you," Taren mumbled when she pulled the door open.

"No, you don't," Gi answered as she walked out.

Taren stomped all the way to her office. In all the years they were together, Gi had never once denied her. Whatever game she was playing, it was cold and completely unlike her. It made Taren want her even more.

"God damn it!" she cursed.

Taren spent the rest of the day snapping at anyone who spoke to her. She wasn't in the mood to be at work, much less down the hall from the woman who was literally driving her crazy. Deciding she couldn't take it anymore, Taren headed over to Gentleman's Rook after lunch, to see the progress.

Bruno and Sergio were cordial to her as usual, but Mario was flirtatious as ever. Pissed at Gi, Taren allowed herself the luxury of flirting back a little more than usual. Mario's eyes seemed to follow her every move.

Taren looked around at all of the old Chicago gangster and speakeasy pictures that hung on the walls. "The place is coming together nicely," she said.

"Yeah. We still have a couple of weeks." Mario stepped closer. "Hey, how is your grandmother?"

"She's good," Taren stated, wondering how he knew about her family emergency.

Mario smiled. "A few of the bills keep coming here instead of the main office," he added. "I was trying to get the addresses changed, but Gi said you'd do it when you got back from visiting your grandmother."

"Oh." Taren smiled. "I'll get it straightened out. Do you have any of them now?"

"Yes," he said, leading her to the manager's office, which was still in disarray. He handed her a small stack of envelopes.

Taren flipped through them.

"Who is this?" she asked, looking at one of the unfamiliar names.

"A new vendor. Since this is a cigar and whiskey bar, we're importing whiskey from all over the world, the same with the cigars."

Taren nodded.

"Would you like to have dinner with me tomorrow night? I can tell you all about our vendors."

"Mario, you know I'm engaged." She smiled and stepped back to put a little more space between them.

"Call it a business meeting." He grinned.

Taren raised an eyebrow. "Thank you, but I can't," she said. "Maybe lunch," she added.

"Great. I look forward to it." He walked her outside. "Looks like it's going to rain," he commented, looking at the sky.

"I could use a cold shower," she whispered to herself.

\*\*\*

Taren was late getting home that night, after spending an extra hour at the gym, running off the pent-up frustration. All she wanted to do was take a long shower and try to get some much-needed sleep. However, Ken had other plans. He'd come home with takeout from one of their favorite places and a bottle of wine.

"Why don't you get cleaned up and I'll put this all together," Ken said, wrinkling his nose at her sweatiness.

"Are you trying to say I stink?" she laughed.

"Of course not. You're just…icky from the gym."

"Icky?" she repeated with a chuckle and walked away.

The cool spray of the shower felt good on her heated skin and muscles. She laughed softly when she thought about Ken and his weird issue with sweat. If he was sweaty, he simply took a shower to wash it away, but if she was sweaty, he found it a huge turn off and stayed away from her. Looking back on their relationship, they'd really never been so deep in the throes of passion that they were dripping sweat. Their sex life was very clean, rather calm, and just enough to get you to the end and call it a night. Part of that was her fault. She never initiated sex with him and simply went along with it when it happened. She loved him and just figured sex was different with everyone, as it had been with the couple of partners she'd had.

Thinking about hot, sweaty sex, made her think about Gi, and that only made her mad. Taren turned the water off and stepped out of the shower, eager to get to that bottle of wine. *Just because sex with Ken isn't hot and sweaty, doesn't men it isn't pleasant,* she thought to herself.

***

The next day, Taren was sporting a headache from the wine and the stress of avoiding Gi around the office. She'd gone most of the day without running into the vixen, when she stepped out of her office to use the restroom and ran into Mario in the hallway.

"Hey," he said with a big smile.

Taren smiled thinly, until she saw Gi come up behind him and lean against the wall, arms crossed.

"Did you get the supply order I sent for Rapture?" he asked.

She nodded, raising her eyebrow at the eyes that gave her the once over. "Why were there two initial orders for GR?" she asked.

"I don't know." He shrugged. "Uncle Bruno did the second one." He stepped a little closer. "I'm free for lunch tomorrow if you want to get together." He winked and added, "We can go over there together and see what's going on...afterwards, if you want."

Gi cleared her throat, making him jump like a scared cat. "Why the fuck am I paying you to manage the inventory for each establishment?" she snapped. "Instead of standing here trying to get your dick wet, you should be at GR finding out what was ordered and why! That's what I pay you for!"

"I…"

"Don't get me some piece of shit excuse, Mario. I don't want to hear it. Do your fucking job or you're gone! *Capisci?*"

Mario hung his head and walked away.

Gi raised an eyebrow and turned her eyes to Taren. "What?" Gi asked.

There were a few other invoices that didn't make sense, but the look in Gi's eyes made Taren too keyed-up to discuss them at the moment. She stepped closer, fighting the urge to kiss her.

Gi's assistant stepped into the hallway, breaking the connection between them and Gi walked away without looking back.

*What the hell are you doing?* Taren chastised herself as she headed to her own office.

# Chapter 17

Taren hadn't seen Gi for two days, so when she noticed her car in the parking lot on Friday, she felt a shiver of excitement, followed by the first signs of a stress headache. She walked inside, towards the elevator and pushed the button. The doors swung open immediately, startling her. Taren gasped when she saw Gi standing inside.

The doors started to close and Gi reached out, stopping them. "Are you going up, or are you just going to stand there?" she questioned.

Taren ran her eyes slowly over the woman in front of her. She sighed audibly as she stepped inside.

As soon as the doors closed, Gi pressed the emergency stop button and stepped in front of her. Taren backed up, bumping herself in the wall.

"I'm getting tired of this cat and mouse game, tesoro," Gi murmured, looking into her eyes.

"You walked away from me, remember?" Taren retorted as her blood began to pulse through her veins.

"What do you want?" Gi asked, meeting her eyes again.

"You," Taren whispered breathlessly.

Gi hit the button again, forcing the doors open. She grabbed Taren's hand and pulled her out of the elevator as she walked towards the front doors of Rapture. The early morning sun assaulted them as Gi headed towards her car, still holding Taren's hand. She deposited her in the passenger seat and stepped around to the driver's side.

\*\*\*

Taren felt like Vickie Vail, riding with Batman through Gotham at breakneck speed as Gi careened through the streets of Chicago without saying a word. They finally came to a stop alongside the curb in front of a three-story greystone building. When she got out, Taren looked around; noticing the same style of old, greystone architecture lined both sides of the road with a few oak trees here and there. From looking at real estate with Ken, Taren could tell this was a very affluent neighborhood, rich with old money.

"Where are we?" Taren asked.

"Does it matter?" Gi answered as she grabbed her hand and headed up the small set of stairs with wrought iron railing.

They came to a stop in front of the corner unit on the end. Gi unlocked the door, and stepped inside, inputting the alarm code. Then, she motioned for Taren to come inside.

The foyer had beautiful marbled tile, which contrasted nicely against the cherry wood floors of the formal living room next to it. A couple of chairs sat near the large bay window, with two more chairs and a couch in front of the fireplace. A beautiful, crème colored rug adorned the floor. The back of the living room had a staircase that led upstairs, and opened into a formal dining room with a long, chocolate brown table sitting on a thick, oriental rug with neutral colors that matched the furniture and walls.

She didn't have time to say anything as Gi led her up to the third floor, which opened into a hallway. She tried to look around at the artwork and pictures on the walls, but was shuffled through double doors at the entrance of the large master bedroom.

A massive, black sleigh-bed with attached nightstands sat along the far wall. A chaise lounge and a pair of matching chairs were near the fireplace on the opposite side of the room, and a large flat screen TV hung over the fireplace.

Gi pulled Taren towards her, kissing her softly at first as she moved her further into the room. Taren kicked off her heels and let her bare feet sink into the luxurious crème carpet.

All thoughts of her surroundings left Taren's head as Gi's mouth moved from her lips, across her jaw and down her neck. She stretched her head back, allowing Gi to trace her tongue in a delicate path, followed by gentle kisses.

Taren gasped when Gi spun her around, keeping the smaller woman in her arms as she brushed her long locks to the side, continuing the soft, teasing kisses on the base of her neck. Taren breathed heavily as she leaned against the warm, solid body behind her.

Gi moved her arms up, caressing Taren's small, perky breasts before releasing the buttons of her blouse one at a time; all without removing her lips from the tender area she knew drove Taren wild. As soon as her shirt was free, Gi pulled it loose, draping it over the chair with her jacket. Taren spun around and grabbed a handful of Gi's short hair, pulling her into a hard kiss.

The rest of their clothes were shed as they traded frantic kisses, biting and suckling each other's lips and tongue. Gi watched as Taren climbed onto the high bed, sitting up on her knees in the middle.

"Come here," Taren murmured with a husky voice.

Gi obliged, and their bodies came together. She pushed Taren to her back and moved on top of her, running her mouth over every inch of the delicate skin around Taren's flat stomach. She dipped lower, sliding her tongue through the wet, hairless folds at the apex of her thighs.

"Yes," Taren moaned, biting her lip as she watched Gi's mouth move over her.

Gi pulled away and moved back up Taren's slender body. Taren rolled Gi to her back and straddled her. Lust-filled blue eyes gazed up at her as Taren's hands moved to her breasts.

Taren grabbed Gi's hands, falling forward and planting them above her head as she rocked her crotch against the woman under her. Gi reveled in the feeling of Taren's soft, wavy locks cascading over her chest as Taren kissed her way down. She ran her hand through them and lifted her hips to meet Taren's mouth.

"Oh, tesoro," she called out as Taren's tongue circled her clit and entered her over and over.

Taren grinded against her and Gi's thighs shuddered as she entered her with two fingers, feeling the thick wetness coat her mouth and hand while continuing the aggressive strokes with her tongue. Gi's body gave way, tightening around her as she climaxed.

"Too soon, baby," Taren growled, raising her eyes to Gi's. She continued moving in and out of her.

Gi gasped breathlessly and pushed herself down, pulling Taren's fingers out of her and sliding the woman over her mouth in a swift motion. Taren planted her thighs firmly on either side of Gi's head as Gi's mouth devoured her.

"Oh, my God!" she swooned, barely able to hold herself up as she rocked back and forth.

Gi rolled her to the side before she could climax. Taren tried to object, but Gi slid two fingers deep inside her and kissed her passionately. Their wet mouths moved together, tasting each other. Taren lifted her hips against the fingers working in and out, harder and harder. Their hot, sweaty bodies slid together.

"Fuck me, Gi," Taren moaned as she kissed her.

Gi pulled her mouth free, moving down to lick her nipples and suck her breasts. Taren threw her head back, enjoying the sensations running through her body.

Gi slowed her fingers when she felt Taren begin to tighten, holding them deep inside as she climaxed. She finally pulled free and rolled away.

Taren watched her get off the bed and start to pull her clothes back on, before getting up and doing the same. She stepped into the beautiful, Italian tile bathroom, looking in the mirror at the reflection of the large garden tub and glass enclosed shower.

Gi walked up to the sink next to her, washing her hands as well.

"This is your house, isn't it?" Taren asked, looking at her in the mirror.

Gi turned off the water and reached for the hand towel below. "We need to get back," she sighed.

"You don't have to be so insensitive," Taren said as she dried her hands and turned around.

Gi pushed her back against the sink, looking directly into her eyes. "This is a purely sexual thing, no pillow talk.

That's what you want, isn't it?" When Taren didn't answer, she walked away.

On her way back downstairs, Taren got a better look at the house. She took a brief peek at the kitchen on the second floor, which had stark white cabinets on top, light grey lower cabinets, stainless appliances, white and gray marbled counter tops, and medium-shaded, hardwood floors. The entire floor had antique crown molding and wide archways with modern décor. Taren felt like she'd stepped into a real estate magazine.

Gi was leaning against the back of the sofa in the formal living room with her arms crossed and her eyebrow raised. Taren stayed quiet as she walked past her and out the front door.

***

Nothing was said as they drove back across town. Taren didn't like this distant, emotionless side of Gi. She'd never seen her so guarded. It was almost scary and completely uncharacteristic for the woman she used to love. As the buildings and streets passed by, Taren began to think about what she'd done. Leaving with Gi that morning hadn't felt like a mistake. Not at all. She'd felt almost carefree. But now, she felt dirty. She looked over at the woman next to her, wanting so desperately to talk to her, but Gi was right. The connection between them was physical. Taren wondered: would the emptiness she felt inside be enough for her to let the past go…let Gi go? Or would she come for more when she craved the connection only Gi could give her?

Taren's thoughts vanished like smoke when the Audi pulled into Rapture's parking lot and rolled to a stop near the front door.

"Aren't you coming in?" Taren asked.

"No. I have to go deal with the fire inspector at GR," Gi answered.

"I thought the new sprinklers were in already."

"They are, but he's being a dick about something else now. I had a voicemail from Sergio."

"Okay," Taren said, not sure what else to say.

"Let me when you want to get away from the office again." Gi winked.

Taren nodded and got out of the car. She stood to the side, watching the black sports car speed off as her mind raced. *What are you doing to me, Gi? Why can't I let you go?*

# *Chapter 18*

Over the next few days, Taren couldn't get Gi and their encounter out of her head. Why had Gi taken her home? To her bed? Why not a hotel, or even the couch for that matter?

When Monday rolled around, Taren couldn't take it any longer. She walked into Gi's office and closed the door.

"Hi," Gi said with a questioning look on her face.

"Can we get out of here?"

Gi shrugged and grinned. "Let's go."

\*\*\*

When they arrived in front of the corner greystone, Taren pulled up alongside the curb behind Gi's car and got out.

"I didn't exactly mean here," she said.

"If not here, then where? A hotel? Your place perhaps?" Gi questioned, unlocking the door.

Taren walked inside and waited for Gi to close the door. "I wasn't referring to sex."

"What do you want to do? Talk?" Gi shook her head, stepping closer. "You said it yourself, nothing personal."

"Damn it, Gi!" Taren growled. "I don't like you like this."

"Like what? A piece of ass on the side? That is what I am, isn't it?"

"I don't know what you are!" Taren shook her head. "I can't…" She sighed, "I can't stop wanting you."

Gi moved closer, backing her up against the wall with a searing kiss that left them both breathless. Taren wrapped her arms around Gi's shoulders, welcoming the demanding kiss, before Gi leaned down, running her hand up under Taren's skirt, between her legs. Taren moved against her, urging her further. Clothes were peeled away as they moved along the walls, finally ending up on the edge of the stairs, as they frantically brought each other to climax, oblivious to their uncomfortable surroundings.

\*\*\*

The next morning, Taren woke up with her back and shoulder blades aching. She stretched her tense muscles in the hot shower and did a little yoga before getting ready for work.

"Where did you get those bruises on your back?" Ken asked, coming up behind her and kissing the marks.

Taren froze.

He'd just returned from one of his morning runs and was rushing around to take a shower and get to work.

"I got hit by a door," she lied. *Oh, my God. A door?* She shook her head realizing she and Gi had never made it off the first floor, or really off the floor at all, during their tryst the day before. They spent most of the two hours tangled together on the stairs and then on the fancy rug in the living room.

"How did that happen?"

"It's my own fault. I was standing in front of the receiving door downstairs when someone came through with a delivery of liquor. I'm fine."

"Wow. Did it knock you down?"

"No. The door just slammed my back. It's fine. I need to get going or I'm going to be late. We have a meeting this morning." She kissed him and finished dressing as he got into the shower.

\*\*\*

Taren was standing in the hallway, talking to Gi's assistant when Uncle Bruno, Sergio, and Mario stepped off the elevator with Gi. She winced, trying to keep her smile as Uncle Bruno put his hand in the middle of her back when he passed by. Sergio smiled politely and Mario stopped to whisper in her ear, as they made their way into Gi's office.

"Are you okay?" Gi asked, noticing the expression on her face.

"My back's bruised," she whispered.

Gi furrowed her brow, then slowly straightened it as images of the previous afternoon filled her head. "How bad is it?"

"Ken noticed a couple of spots."

Gi rolled her eyes. "What did Mario say to you?" she asked, changing the subject.

"He keeps trying to get me to do with him what I'm doing with you."

"That fucking weasel!" Gi hissed.

"What?" Uncle Bruno said, turning towards the doorway where Gi and Taren were talking.

"Nothing," Gi answered, walking into the room and taking a seat in one of the chairs opposite the couch her family was sitting on.

Taren sat in the chair next to her.

"So, we're officially a week away from the grand opening. How are the new hires working out?" Gi asked, looking at Sergio.

"Great," he replied.

"Marketing?"

"We have ads running in all of the major entertainment booklets, flyers up at all of the country clubs, and we sent out a press release," Sergio added.

"I think we're ready," Uncle Bruno grinned.

"Now that the fire marshal is off our ass, we should pass the final inspection tomorrow. My assistant sent out the invitations for the VIP party the night before the opening. So far, twenty of them have responded with a plus one, and I think maybe ten will be alone."

"How many did you send out?" Sergio asked.

"Fifty total, which would put us at a hundred, plus all of us. The capacity is 300, so we'll be good," Gi answered. "Mario, get with the catering company to make sure we don't need to do anything beforehand. The last thing we need is a food issue. Also, I know the supply orders came in a week ago, but what about the order we placed for VIP night?"

"We got the cigars yesterday and the liquor should be in Monday at the latest," he replied.

"Keep me updated. I'm sure some guests won't want whiskey, so we need to make sure we get that order." Gi looked at her notebook. "Sergio, make sure Taren gets the invoices for all of the advertising. She needs to update the budget before she can bring the new establishment live in the system."

"I'll get it to you today," he said in Taren's direction.

"Thanks," she nodded.

"Uncle Bruno, make sure everything is polished to a mirrored shine. If that cleaning crew isn't good enough, get another one in there. Besides that, I think we're looking good. I'll be there in the morning to meet Inspector Dickhead. He should be in a good mood after our meeting last week."

"Sounds good," Uncle Bruno laughed.

As everyone moved to leave, Mario stepped over to Taren again. Gi watched him wrap his arm around her waist. Taren smiled politely before walking towards her own office.

"Sergio," Gi called down the hall, waving him back to her.

"Yeah," he said, telling his dad to go on.

"You better get Mario off Taren and onto something else. If he puts his hands on her again, I'm going to rip his dick off and feed it to him," she growled.

Sergio shook his head. "He's young and dumb."

"That's not my problem. I agreed to let Uncle Bruno in on my business, but Mario wasn't part of the deal. My hiring him…that was just me being nice. I don't feel so nice anymore."

"I'll get him in line. Pop doesn't need to know he's being stupid."

Gi shrugged.

"Is there something with you and Taren?"

"I didn't put that rock on her finger," Gi replied.

"I know that…but—"

"Taren is an employee. I'll not have any of my employees sexually harassed. That's all you need to be concerned about."

Sergio nodded. "I'll get it taken care of."

Gi waited for him to walk away, before stepping into Taren's office.

"How bad is your back? Let me see it."

"I'm fine, and since when are you compassionate? I thought it was just sex." Taren pinned her with a stare.

"Fine." Gi threw her hands up. "I can't get anything right with you."

"What's that supposed to mean?"

"First, you say nothing personal. Then, I'm too crass. Now, we're drawing a line in the sand again." Gi shook her head. "Send up a flare or smoke signal when you want me again," she huffed.

"Gi…you know it's not like that." Taren moved closer, placing her hand on Gi's cheek. "You and I…we have so much more than history between us." She shook her head and sighed. "It's complicated."

"Anyway, I didn't mean to put you on the spot. I actually came in here to tell you Mario won't be propositioning you anymore. And if he does, I want to know about it right away."

"What did you do?" Taren asked cautiously.

"Nothing."

"Uh huh," Taren laughed.

"Lunch today?" Gi winked.

"No." Taren said. "I have too much to do around here. You know you actually pay me to work here, right?"

"I'll be busy tomorrow with GR."

"What about Friday?"

118

Gi thought for a second, mentally going through her calendar. "Friday works for me. Let's just meet at the house, say one o'clock?"

"It's a date." Taren grinned.

As soon as Gi walked out of the room, Taren flopped down in her desk chair and put her head in her hands. "So much for getting Gi out of your system. Now, you're planning hook-ups with her," she said to herself.

\*\*\*

After dinner, Taren relaxed on the couch in front of the TV. Ken handed her a glass of wine when he walked in, sitting down next to her.

"My mother keeps asking if we've set a date." He smiled, patting her thigh.

"I hadn't thought much about it," she said honestly. "My mind has been going in a hundred directions lately."

"I thought taking this new job would alleviate some of your stress," he said. "I don't think you've slept a full night in two months."

She knew he was right. She hadn't been sleeping well, but it wasn't because of her job. Her past with Gi had haunted her dreams from the beginning, and now their current encounters were invading her sleep.

"Things will get better once the new bar opens," she reassured him.

"I hope so."

Taren finished her wine and set the glass on the table. "How about sometime next fall?" said softly.

Ken shrugged. "That's a year away."

"It takes a while to plan a wedding and California summers are too damn hot."

"That makes sense. I'll tell we're looking at next October?" He shrugged, looking at her for approval.

"Sure." Taren smiled.

"Will I get to meet the infamous Gi at the VIP party next week?" he asked.

"She'll be there," Taren raised an eyebrow.

"Good. I plan to tell her to quit working my fiancé so hard; she has a wedding to plan." He smiled.

Taren nearly dumped wine into her lap as she choked on the sip she'd just swallowed.

"Are you okay?" he asked, grabbing her glass and patting her back.

"Yeah...fine...went down...the wrong pipe," she coughed and sputtered, trying to get the wine out of her lungs. "I think I'm going to go to bed and try to catch up on some sleep."

"Are you sure you're all right?"

Taren kissed his cheek. "Yes."

"I'm going to watch the rest of the news."

She nodded and walked into the kitchen to place her wine glass in the sink.

"I love you," he called out.

"Love you, too," she replied.

# *Chapter 19*

Taren rolled to her back, covered in sweat and sated from a rigorous hour and a half in bed. She stared up at the vaulted ceiling, catching her breath as her body began to relax.

"What made you buy this place?" she asked, turning her head to the side.

"I fell in love with the mixture of modern style and antique architecture," Gi replied, getting out of the bed to get dressed.

"Will you show me around?" Taren asked softly, rolling to her side.

Gi looked down at her. Taren's tan skin contrasted against the light gray sheets and her long, wavy hair cascaded across the pillow behind her. She had a questioning look in her hazel eyes and a thin smile on her delicate lips.

"I thought you had to get back," Gi answered.

"Ken's usually gone most of the day when he plays golf," Taren replied, finally getting out of bed to redress.

Gi nodded and walked into the bathroom to wash her hands and face.

"You don't have to," Taren murmured, stepping up to the other sink to do the same.

"Come on," Gi said, grabbing her when she finished. The first place they went was through the French doors that led to the wide, square patio with modern furniture and a beautiful view.

"This is stunning. I'd be out here every night, looking at the stars."

"I actually thought about you and your love of the stars the first time I came out here at night," Gi murmured.

They walked across the master bedroom when they stepped back inside, through another door that opened into a large walk-in closet with four hanging areas, two built-in dressers, and a floor-to-ceiling mirror.

"Holy shit!" Taren exclaimed with a smile. "Who has this many clothes?"

Gi laughed and took her out of the master bedroom. Next were a library and a home office. It was long and slim with dark cherry floors and a matching antique bookcase that lined one whole wall. The walls were painted bluish-gray. A dark brown, leather chaise and a matching chair with an ottoman were in front of the corner fireplace. The other end of the room had a rolltop desk and an old-fashioned, wingback chair.

"Who is that?" she asked, pointing to the pictures along the wall.

"These are my great-grandfather and grandfather with the Outfit. That one over here is the ship they came over on from Italy when they immigrated."

"Wow."

"This is sort of my historical room."

"I'm still floored by your family history," Taren admitted.

"Did you think I was lying to you?" Gi grinned.

Taren shook her head. "You know how someone catches a fish and by the time they've told ten people, they caught a shark? I just figured you inflated your family's story a little bit."

Gi laughed and took her hand, leading her further down the hall opposite the master bedroom. "These two are spare bedrooms," she said, showing them briefly, before heading down to the second floor.

"This kitchen is definitely fit for a chef," Taren beamed, walking through the long space to the breakfast nook in the back. "Do you still cook?"

Gi shrugged. "Not much. I live alone, so…"

"Is the kitchen the only thing on this floor?"

"No." Gi motioned for her to follow as she went down the hallway.

The room on the front of the house opened into den with an L-shaped, worn, leather couch and matching ottoman that took up most of the room. Pictures cluttered the walls and thick, Berber carpet covered the floor. A huge entertainment center sat along the wall.

Taren grinned. "This looks more like you," she laughed, walking around.

"Yeah, I can't live without my woman-cave." Gi smiled.

"Our entire apartment in L.A. was a damn woman-cave. It looked a lot like this, actually." Taren shook her head. "These are beautiful," she said, looking at the pictures.

"Thanks. I took them while I was living in Paris and Milan."

"When did you get into photography?" Taren asked.

Gi shrugged. "I wasn't really. I wanted to remember the things and places that meant the most to me while I was in Paris, so I took a bunch of photos. They came out amazingly, so when I went to live in Milan, I did the same thing."

"How long did you live there?"

"Milan or Paris?"

"Both. What made you travel internationally to begin with?"

Gi leaned against the back of the couch and crossed her arms. "When you left me, nothing felt right anymore. I was sort of in limbo. That's when JW made me an offer to buy the gambling ring. I took it and graduated with my master's a few weeks later. The day after graduation, I went to the airport to go home to Chicago and wound up on a plane bound for Paris."

Taren nodded, unsure what to say. That hadn't been the best time for her either.

"I stayed in France for a about a year, mostly in Paris."

"What did you do there?"

"The same thing as everyone else. I ate food I couldn't pronounce and toured a lot of neat places. I also made some friends who introduced me to the underworld. I spent a lot of time in night clubs, rubbing arms with people from all over the world. I wound up running a few girls and made a little money." She shrugged.

"You were a pimp?" Taren raised an eyebrow.

"No. It was more of an escort service with a la carte benefits."

"Seriously?" Taren exclaimed.

"Yeah. It didn't last long, maybe four months. I'd already moved on when my dad got sick and I came home."

Taren nodded. "How did you wind up in Milan?"

"I didn't handle my dad's death very well," Gi sighed. "I took off to Tokyo, wanting to be away from everything. Anyway, after a couple of weeks, I met a girl who was traveling to Milan. I accompanied her and wound up staying for a year and a half."

"With her?"

Gi shook her head. "That ended within weeks of our arrival."

Taren bit her lower lip. "Did you run women there, too?"

"No. I got back into selling drugs."

Taren crossed her arms. "So you became an international criminal after I left."

"Pretty much," Gi sighed.

"Why did you leave Milan?"

"My suppliers started pushing guns. I hadn't intended on getting back into selling drugs to begin with, so when that happened, I guess I woke up. I walked away and booked my flight home the same day." She pushed off the back of the couch. "I dumped my entire savings into R&R, and you know the rest."

"You've come a long way from that college girl who wore ripped jeans and t-shirts, and lived in a one bedroom apartment." Taren smiled, shaking her head. "I still find it hard to believe you're a law-abiding citizen now."

Gi pushed off the back of the couch. "I finally found something to love as much as I loved you." She paused. "You know R&R is the acronym for Rapture and Rogue, but it was all inspired by Revisi and Rauley." She smiled softly. "You're the reason I'm where I am today," she sighed, "though I never expected to see you again."

Taren's chest ached at the sentiment. "Gi…" she whispered, looking into the deep blue eyes staring back at her.

Gi moved closer, closing the gap between them. Taren's cell phone rang loudly, severing the moment before their lips could meet. She froze when she saw the caller ID and Gi walked away, knowing who it was without asking.

"Hey," she answered with a soft tone.

"Where are you?" he asked. "I just finished playing golf and was hoping to take you to Marcella's for dinner. I know you've been stressed and my hounding you about the wedding probably isn't helping."

"It's fine. I'm actually at the office right now."

"On a Sunday?"

"Yeah. I forgot to send out the press release Friday for the VIP party," she lied. "I'm leaving now, though. Marcella's sounds good."

"Okay. I'll get in the shower then."

"See you soon." Taren ended the call and shoved the phone into her back pocket.

Gi was standing in the kitchen, drinking a glass of water when Taren walked in. She stepped closer and Gi set the glass in the sink, before turning away from her and walking towards the staircase. Taren hung her head and followed.

# *Chapter 20*

Twenty-four hours before the new bar's grand opening, Taren noticed one of the company accounts was missing nearly a hundred thousand dollars. She looked everywhere, trying to find invoices to match the discrepancy, and finally ran across a couple of new receipts that had been added under Gentlemen's Rook. The vendors didn't match anything in the system, so it was flagging as an error. Unsure who the vendor was, Taren called Gi to confirm since she was over at the new bar.

"That name doesn't ring a bell with me," Gi said. "It's probably something to do with the press release or VIP party. Go ahead and put it through to reconcile the account."

"Are you sure? Gi, it's close to a hundred grand and it was removed from an account that isn't linked to GR."

"Yeah. It's fine. Don't worry about it. I'm sure everything will straighten out in a week or two."

Taren hung up the phone and shook her head as she corrected the error. Something about the miscalculation didn't sit well with her. Gi knew the business inside and out, so she had to trust her judgment, but it still bothered Taren knowing she was missing important details.

***

Gentleman's Rook was bustling with people and music when Taren and Ken walked inside. Taren hadn't seen it since its completion and the place looked like a large, bi-level speakeasy with a long bar against the side wall and vintage style leather chairs and smoking tables throughout. Everything was dark wood and aged-whiskey-colored, with old pictures all over the walls. It was like stepping into the 1920s. They'd done a great job matching the time period.

A jazz band was playing low music in one corner, and the caterer was set up in another with tables full of food. People mingled about, sipping cocktails and discussing everything from the new bar to who was running in the next election.

"This place is nothing like I expected," Ken said. "I guess I couldn't picture it when you described it."

"It's changed even more since I last saw it," Taren replied. "If you were a whiskey and cigar man, is this somewhere you'd go?"

"I don't know, maybe." Ken smiled. "I hope they have more to drink than whiskey."

Taren laughed. "Tonight yes, but once it opens officially, no. They have fifty different whiskey brands from all over the world though, which is why those women are walking around with mini-shots. Free samples," She explained. "Do you want a drink?"

Ken nodded and they walked over to the bar, each getting a glass of wine. Taren noticed Gi at the end of the bar, wearing an expensive suit and sipping a glass of whiskey. She was talking to Uncle Bruno and a few other men who looked as much like mobsters as Gi's uncle had when she'd first met him.

Taren and Ken had barely taken a sip of their drinks when Uncle Bruno appeared.

"What do you think?" Uncle Bruno asked with a big smile on his face.

"I can't believe how different it looks," Taren gushed. "I love it." She smiled in Gi's direction as she walked by.

Gi eyed the man standing with his arm around Taren's waist as she moved past them to get a refill of her drink.

"Ken, this is Gi's uncle—"

"Bruno," he said, sticking his hand out. "You must be the fiancé."

"Yes." Ken smiled.

"Speaking of my niece," Bruno said, patting Gi's back.

Gi smiled at her uncle and turned to see Ken staring at her.

"Gianna Revisi," she said, holding her hand out to him.

"Ken Myer," he replied with a smile.

"The place looks great," Taren said.

"Thanks." Gi nodded. "If you'll excuse me, I need to mingle. It was nice meeting you, Ken. Taren, would you like to meet some of our business associates?" she added.

"Sure," Taren shrugged.

"I won't keep her long." Gi grinned at him. "Help yourself to the food and whatever you want to drink."

"What was that about?" Taren asked when she walked away with Gi's hand on the small of her back.

"Some of our vendors are here, as well as the mayor and a state senator. I thought you'd like to meet them."

Taren nodded.

\*\*\*

A little while later, Taren returned, having met enough people for one night. Ken watched Gi move through the crowd, towards a pretty blond in a skimpy dress. "She's not what I expected at all," he murmured.

Following his line of sight, Taren watched Gi kiss the woman's cheek, before moving on to someone else.

"She's somewhat of a ladies woman, isn't she?" he mumbled.

"Huh?" Taren watched Gi move around the room.

"Gi. It's hard to picture you two as friends in college."

"We were different people back then," she sighed.

\*\*\*

An hour later, Taren walked out of the back bathroom, having used it since the front one was packed with VIP guests. Gi walked out of the office, talking and laughing with the blond Taren had seen her with earlier. She raised an eyebrow and crossed her arms.

"Hey." Gi walked over to her. "I was about to come find you."

"Really?" Taren eyed her.

"Vivian, this is Taren Rauley, our Financial Director," Gi said. "Taren, this is Vivian Sanders."

"It's nice to meet you." She smiled. "Gianna, a pleasure to see you as always," she said, kissing Gi's cheek. "The place looks great."

"Thanks." Gi smiled.

Gi turned to Taren, who looked like she was trying to strangle Gi with her pretty, hazel eyes.

"Care to explain?" Taren questioned in a low voice. "Who the hell was that? One of your floozies?"

"My what?" Gi asked, taken aback. "What business is it of yours?"

"If you're messing with other people, I think I have a right to know," Taren growled. "I don't want to catch something from you."

Gi's jaw stiffened. "You have a lot of nerve. It's not like you're going home alone every night. I don't know where his dick's been!"

"That's low, even for you."

Gi grabbed Taren's hand and pulled her into the office, backing her up against the closed door. "First of all, I haven't been with anyone but you since this thing between us started. I'm not the one having an affair while I'm engaged to someone else!" When Taren tried to talk, Gi shushed her. "Second, if you'd let me explain, you'd have found out that Vivian is the mayor's assistant. I'm pretty sure she's fucking him, but that's not the point. I brought her in here because I promised I'd donate to his new campaign if she got him to come tonight as a guest; I wrote her a check from this company's account."

Taren wasn't sure what to say.

Gi backed away, shaking her head.

\*\*\*

Later that night, Taren sat on the couch with the blinds open, listening to the rain and thunder, and watching the lightning brighten the sky as a nasty thunderstorm passed over. She'd been unable to sleep and wound up on the couch sometime around two in the morning.

She kept replaying the night over in her head. She'd been so jealous and mad as a wet hen when she'd seen Gi with Vivian. Even worse was the fact that Gi was right. She really didn't have a say. How could she be jealous when she was the one having an affair? It wasn't like she and Gi had made any kind of commitment to each other. In fact, they hadn't really talked about what was going on between them. The only thing they both knew for certain was their physical connection was just as strong as it had been five years ago.

Taren wiped a tear from her cheek as the sky lit up once again, followed by a loud crack of thunder. She didn't want to hurt Ken; she loved him. At the same time, she couldn't deny the attraction to Gi, the woman she once loved more than anything in the world.

*Do you ever really stop loving someone?*

# Chapter 21

The week after the new bar opened, the stress of juggling her life with Ken and her affair with Gi was driving Taren crazy. She'd tried to end it with Gi, but she couldn't. Gi was like a drug. When they were together, the high was extreme. When they were apart, the sober life was nice, too. But the high was always in the back of her mind.

She was exhausted when she got home from the office at night and when they had dinner, she pushed the food around until it looked like she'd eaten.

Finally, one night, Ken sat down on the couch and put his arm around her.

"Are you pregnant?" he asked.

Taren pulled away from him like he was a stranger. "Excuse me?"

Ken shrugged. "Howard, one of the guys in my office, said his wife started acting weird, stressed out, couldn't sleep, wasn't eating, and it turned out she was pregnant."

"No," Taren said, "I am most definitely not pregnant."

"Okay, then what's going on? Is it something with Gi?"

"What?"

"I noticed you two were pretty chummy at the party last week. There's more to you knowing her in college, isn't there?"

"What do you mean?"

"Did you two party harder than most people? Or were maybe good friends and had a falling out?"

"What? Gi and I were barely friends in college."

"I don't know. You're acting different. It's like you've become a completely different person since you went to work for her.

"It's just stress." She patted his thigh. "I have a lot on my plate right now, that's all."

"I understand stress, Taren. I handle billion dollar acquisitions for a living. Whatever is going on with you is much worse." He wrapped his arm around her. "Maybe you should see a therapist or go to a spa, find a way to relax and let work go."

"I don't need a shrink," she laughed. "But a spa day does sound really good. I think I will book an appointment for this weekend."

"Good. You're not yourself lately and I'm really starting to worry about you."

"I'll be fine," she said, kissing him softly.

\*\*\*

The following Monday, Taren sat at her desk, feeling refreshed from spending Saturday at the day spa, rejuvenating herself and her mind. She'd gone the entire day without seeing Gi, which was a good thing.

Her high lasted until she noticed another chunk of money missing from one of the accounts they used to pay the suppliers. She started looking at the ledger for that account. There were no withdrawals, and none of the supply order invoices matched the amount.

Taren immediately grabbed the phone and dialed Gi's cell number.

"Hey," Gi answered.

"Are you coming back to the office?" Taren asked.

"No. It's five. You should be heading home," Gi replied, shifting gears as she came to a stop in the downtown traffic.

"I found another error, this time it's with our supply account. Something's going on."

"I'm headed to my house. Come over. I'll make you dinner and we can talk about what you found."

"I need to be able to get into the accounts to show you everything."

"You know we have access to our server remotely, right?" Gi asked.

"Yes. I guess…I don't know. I've never trusted a remote system."

"It's fine. I do it all the time."

"All right. I'll see you in a little bit. Do I need to bring anything?" Taren asked.

"Dessert," Gi teased, and hung up.

*** 

Taren leaned against the counter, watching Gi sauté shrimp to add to the pasta primavera she was cooking.

"You can open a bottle of wine if you want. There are reds and whites in the cooler." Gi nodded towards the built-in wine cooler on the other side of the dishwasher.

"I'm fine." Taren sighed. "Since when do you drink wine?"

Gi laughed. "I keep it for company."

Taren smiled and shook her head. "It's definitely an acquired taste." She looked around at the immaculate kitchen. "When's the last time you cooked in here? It looks like nothing has ever been touched."

"I don't know, six months, maybe." She shrugged.

"Where do you eat?"

Gi raised an eyebrow.

"Come here," she said, holding a spoonful of the sauce she had simmering on the back burner.

Taren moved closer, allowing Gi to touch her lips with the spoon. "Ohhh," she cooed, "that's good!"

Gi grinned. "It's almost done. Grab the plates from that cabinet."

When Taren set the plates on the counter, Gi went to work mixing all of the ingredients and adding a generous portion to each plate. She topped off both dishes with a sprinkle of cheese, and set the plates on the small table in the breakfast nook.

"This is amazing," Taren exclaimed, tasting her first full bite.

"Thanks. Sometimes I forget how much better food is when you cook it yourself."

"I'm surprised you eat out so much. You always cooked in college."

Gi shrugged. "I had someone to cook for."

\*\*\*

When they'd finished dinner, Gi tossed everything in the dishwasher and moved closer to Taren, pinning her to the counter she was leaning against. Their lips met softly, sending a throbbing pain to the middle of Taren's chest. She casually pushed Gi away.

"We need to talk about what's going on with the supply account," she murmured.

"Is that really what you want to do? Discuss numbers?" Gi whispered, kissing her again.

Taren felt her knees grow weak. She wrapped her arms around Gi's neck, reveling in the intoxicating sensation of Gi's mouth against hers. She squeezed her eyes closed, forgetting all about accounting as Gi's hips moved against hers in a slow, seductive motion.

The ringing of Taren's phone shattered the moment. Taren pulled away to answer it.

Gi went upstairs to the library to boot up the computer on her desk. She sat in the large, wingback chair, staring at the full bookcase, while she waited for it to connect to the company server.

Taren appeared a few minutes later. "Sorry," she said. "That was Ken. He left this morning for Cleveland."

Gi rolled her eyes, realizing that was why Taren had agreed to dinner. She logged into the system and turned around. "Where is the issue?"

Taking Ken's phone call had been a huge mistake. Taren knew should've sent it to voicemail. Her body was still reeling from the make-out session in the kitchen, which was heading towards sex right there against the counter. She'd barely been able to hold the conversation with him out of guilt for what he'd interrupted. She glanced around the room, trying to clear her head.

"Where is the issue?" Gi asked again, with a slightly harsher tone in her voice.

"Supplies. Go to the bank statement for the supply account," Taren replied, looking over her shoulder.

"These are all vendor orders," Gi stated.

"That one isn't." Taren pointed to a transfer of $98,400.

Gi went into the supply ledger, looking for any recent amounts that would add up to the transfer, but nothing matched. "This has to be Uncle Bruno or Sergio using the wrong account to pay for something." She shook her head.

"What the hell cost nearly a hundred grand? The bar has been open for two weeks."

"It could be an old invoice from the renovation. It's really not a big deal, Taren."

"Why does your family have so much access to your company? You used to never trust anyone."

"It can't do it all alone. Part of bringing my uncle into the business was allowing him access to be able to run GR on his own eventually. I had to make sure he was capable of that."

Taren rolled her eyes.

"You disagree?" Gi asked, leaning her elbow on the arm of the chair and resting her chin on the top of her closed fist.

"I don't know. It's not my money, or my company. So, I really have no place to say anything," Taren sighed, looking into the blue eyes fixated on her. The emotional rollercoaster she was riding was too much for her to handle, and the fact that Gi could care less about the missing money was starting to make Taren think she'd made an even bigger mistake going to work for her.

"Don't tell me you still think I'm laundering money." Gi turned the computer off and shook her head.

"You have access to everything, including my personal bank accounts."

Taren's phone rang again and she reached for it without answering Gi.

"How much longer are you going to keep your little secret?" Gi asked, raising her eyebrow.

"Huh?" Taren looked down at the phone, seeing Ken's picture.

"When are you going to tell him you've been having cake and eating it, too?"

Taren sent the call to her voicemail. "Are you serious?" she growled.

"I want to know. How much longer are you going to play him for a fool? Or is me you've been playing all this time?"

"It's complicated."

"No, it's not. In fact, it's quite simple. You came back to me, so why are you still with him? Or is this just a torrid affair to give you the thrills you're missing at home?" Gi sneered.

"Damn it, Gi, stop!"

"I'm trying to figure this all out. He has to know something is going on. It's eating away at you. I see it every time I look into your eyes."

"He does and he's asked." Taren shook her head, trying to avoid the tears. "Look, I can't do this right now, okay?"

"Why did you come back to me?"

"I don't know," Taren huffed. "I thought I could get you out of my system."

"And how is that working for you?" Gi crossed her arms.

"You really want to know?" Taren threw her hands up. "It's killing me! My life was good before you came back into it! I was happy!" she yelled.

"I wasn't exactly looking for you either. You came into *my* bar. I had no idea where you were or what you were doing. Five god damn years, Taren! You left me...remember? You came back into *my* life!"

"You offered me the job!"

"You didn't have to take it! I offered it because I needed your skills!"

Taren clenched her jaw and looked away. "Don't say you didn't want something to happen."

"Well, don't tell me you were happy, because if you were, you wouldn't have started this," Gi's voice softened. "You wouldn't have come back to me."

"We..." Taren sighed. "This thing between us...Gi, it's unhealthy. It's making me crazy. You make me crazy."

Gi nodded. "Well, let me help you out. I'm done." She shrugged. "I'll make the choice for you. You go home to Ken and ride his dick all you want. All I care about is the work you do for my company. If that's too much for you and you want to go, I'll even give you severance." She opened the drawer of the desk and removed her check book, barely able to contain the emotions she was hiding from Taren as she filled out the slip.

Taren wiped a tear from her cheek.

Gi handed her the check. "Go, Taren, be happy and never come back, because I won't be here," Gi growled, choosing anger over the sadness of feeling her heart break again over this woman.

# *Chapter 22*

Taren spent the rest of the night and all of the next day crying. She was thankful Ken was out of town because she truly had no explanation for him, other than the truth. She cried for the mistake she made starting the affair, the pain of losing Gi again, and the thought of not knowing what she wanted anymore. The sadness finally turned to anger a day later, making Taren raging mad. She turned to blaming Gi for everything from their getting together, to her simply pushing Taren away like a bad habit. The more she thought about the last two months, the more pissed she became. She'd never intended on starting an affair with Gi, but it had become so much more than that.Even though she'd been unable to say it, she was sure Gi felt it, too. She couldn't throw everything away, not again, and she wondered how Gi could so easily. Had she actually been making a fool of Taren, getting back at the woman who'd broken her heart? There had to be a reason Gi turned on her, ending everything like it had been nothing at all.

Taren's mind turned to the account discrepancies that she kept finding, making her wonder if she had found something and Gi pushed her away to keep her from uncovering it. If Gi had truly had an issue with Taren still seeing Ken, then why even start the affair? The company books had been a mess and Taren spent weeks putting everything into a nice and neat, efficient system, just as she'd done with the gambling ring.

Thinking she'd been used for Gi's personal gain, Taren lost it. She grabbed the vase from the table and smashed it against the wall. It shattered into a hundred small pieces. The fake flowers and clear marbles in the bottom flew across the room, scattering all over the floor.

"Damn you, Gianna Revisi!" she yelled. "You can bet your ass I'm going to find out what you're up to!"

Taren immediately opened her personal laptop and tried logging into the company. Sure enough, her passwords were still active. She quickly began looking through Gi's personal financial records, comparing them to the company's tax statements for each year since the company had been established.

\*\*\*

By the time Ken arrived home that night, Taren had cleaned up the mess from the vase and gotten through the entire first year of business for R&R. So far, she hadn't found any inconsistencies. She was starting to wonder if she should just let it all go.

"Are you still working?" he asked, walking behind her at the dining table where she had a stack of handwritten notes next to the laptop.

"Actually, I'm not working…well, not technically, anyway." Taren shut down the computer and tucked her notes into a nice little pile. "I lost my job," she said.

"What?"

"The stress was just too much for me. There is way more involved with being the financial director for that company than I ever thought possible," she sighed.

"You'll find something else," Ken said, rubbed her shoulders. He bent down, kissing her cheek. "Do what makes you happy."

Taren watched him walk over to the couch. She had no idea what made her happy anymore. So much had changed. Before they moved to Chicago, Taren was happy and enjoying the life she was living. She was content because in the back of her mind, she knew she'd never see Gianna Revisi again. Keeping Gi out of her sight, also kept her off her mind. It was simple.

Moving to Chicago had been a huge adjustment in itself, but running into Gi had sent her mind on a whirlwind. The past had come rushing back, sweeping Taren off her feet and right into Gi's arms. Reuniting with her had been a living hell and a beautiful dream all at the same time. For the past two months, Taren had been on the most stressful ride of her life, juggling her job, her affair, and her quaint life at home. She should've been happy when Gi did what she couldn't. She put a wall up between them.

Looking at Ken, lounging on the couch, flipping through the channels, she knew what life was like with him: predictable, easy, a steady course. Was that still enough? This was the question she asked herself as she sat down next to him.

\*\*\*

Desperate for something, anything, to justify everything that had happened over the past two months, Taren kept exploring R&R's records, almost to the point of obsession. She spent the rest of the week copying everything onto her computer in case the system caught up with her termination.

A week after everything had blown up between her and Gi, Taren stumbled across the first variation in the accounts. They'd started appearing six months ago. Taren made notes of bank transfers and withdrawals that didn't match any invoices or side notes.

When she began adding these transactions line by line, she realized the money was steadily going out of R&R and nothing additional was coming in.

They're losing money, not gaining," she whispered. "What the hell is going on?"

Taren noticed a lot of money was moving around within the direct accounts for Gentlemen's Rook, way more money than was moving through the other two, well-established businesses. It didn't make sense. There was no way the bar could justify the expenses.

Taren went onto the bank website, praying her login still worked. "Gi, what the hell happened to your trust issues?" she murmured when she was able to get right into the accounts with no problem.

When she clicked on the first transfer in her notes, the money had gone from a fixtures account for Rapture, into the expense account for GR. The next transaction was out of a rollover account for all three businesses, again moved into the GR account. Over the course of the last six months, over a million dollars had been moved out of various accounts all over R&R and deposited into various expense accounts for GR.

"Son of a bitch!" she yelled, when she began digging through the GR accounts. The money was being withdrawn in small increments that wouldn't raise any red flags. None of the withdrawals were listed in the ledger anywhere, meaning the withdrawals weren't used to pay invoices billed to the company.

Taren had no idea what to do. She needed to figure out where the money was going before she could go to Gi. If she was doing something illegal, her bank account should've been growing with money that was unaccounted for. Instead, all of the deposits to her personal account were linked directly to payroll.

The only thing Taren could think of was maybe an offshore account, which she knew Gi had. That was part of the reason they'd vacationed in Mexico and the Cayman Islands. Gi had accounts in both countries where she hid the money she made from the gambling ring. That had been the main reason why the university and local police couldn't crack her system. They were unable to find anything linked to her.

Taren shook her head. Why would Gi steal her own money? It didn't make sense. She was about to start looking at company employees when she heard the front door to the apartment. She looked up to see Ken's smiling face.

"How was your day?" he asked.

"Actually, it was quite interesting," she replied, getting up to hug him.

"Oh, really? Did you find any good prospects?" he asked, hugging her. "Larry's wife works for the hospital system. He said they're always looking for account managers. I gave him your number for her."

*Great,* she thought. *Just what I've always wanted to do.* "No, I think I figured what's going on at R&R. The reason I kept find all of those variances that were stressing me out."

"Who cares?" Ken said, removing his tie and jacket.

"I do. I busted my ass for that company and I knew something was going on. I'm pretty sure Gi's uncle is extorting money from her and using the new bar to cover it up. He's moving amounts that are too small for her to notice, and like a fool, she went away from her golden rule and trusted her family when she shouldn't have."

"Why are you so infatuated with Gianna Revisi? She fired you," he said, annoyed. "I figured you'd be looking at this time to start planning our wedding. But she and that business are all you talk about!"

Taren had rarely heard him raise his voice and it was never towards her, until now. He was always gentle and easygoing. She got up from the table, facing him squarely.

"She didn't fire me," Taren corrected.

"What?"

"I said, she didn't fire me." Taren looked him in the eyes. "She gave me a choice…and then made my decision for me," she sighed.

"What the hell does that mean?"

"I'm sorry, Ken. I have to go back."

"Back to what? Working for that company made you crazy. You're better off away from there. Just let it go."

"I can't." Taren squeezed her eyes shut and held her breath, realizing in that moment that she wasn't where she wanted to be. The picture she saw behind her closed lids wasn't Ken. It was Gi's sexy grin and deep blue gaze calling to her. Taren felt rooted to the ground as she opened her eyes again. "Gianna Revisi makes me lose my mind and God knows we're toxic together," She shook her head. "But, no matter how hard I try…I can't let go of her. I'm sorry."

"What are you saying?" he asked.

Taren took a deep breath and let it out slowly. "Gi and I were together for four years. I should've told you and I'm sorry I didn't. I never thought I'd see her again," she said honestly.

"Wait. What?" He scrunched his brow. "Together? Like…lesbians?" he whispered.

"Yes. I've been in love with her since I was eighteen years old. No matter how hard I tried, I couldn't…I can't…stop loving her. She's where I belong."

Ken shook his head in disbelief. "Are you serious?"

Taren nodded.

"How long have you been screwing her behind my back?" He shouted. "No wonder you were so stressed out. It's not easy hiding your affair with your boss from your fiancé!"

"It doesn't matter. There's nothing to fight for anymore. It's over between you and me." She slipped her ring off and placed it on the table. "I will always care for you, but I'll never love anyone the way I love her." She touched his cheek as she walked past him.

"That's it? You're just going to walk out?" Ken said, shocked.

"There's nothing else to do. Goodbye." She looked around at the few material things that were theirs. All of their furniture and larger belongings were back in San Diego in storage. "I'll get my stuff out of the storage the next time I'm home," she added, packing her clothes and laptop into two suitcases. Then she walked out the door.

Taren was scared to death, yet she had this huge feeling of euphoria, like a heavy flow of adrenaline rushing through her body as she walked to her car. *I hope you know what you're doing*, she thought to herself.

# *Chapter 23*

Taren stood nervously on the doorstep of the large greystone, having just rung the doorbell. She took a deep breath, bouncing from foot to foot while she waited. The dark-colored Audi with tinted windows was parked alongside the curb—a good indication that its owner was home.

After another minute, the deadbolt on the door clicked and the knob turned. Taren held her breath.

"Taren?" Gi questioned with an odd expression.

"Can we talk?"

"I don't really have anything to say to you," Gi sighed. "I told you to never come back and I meant it."

"I choose you," Taren said softly, stepping closer.

"You're too late. I chose for you, remember?" Gi moved to close the door and Taren shoved it open.

"You don't make decisions for me. I said, I choose you."

"I'm not doing this again." Gi shook her head. "What gives you the right to enter and exit my life as you please?" she growled. "You said I make *you* crazy...you have no fucking idea!"

"I left Ken." Taren stepped further into the foyer, closing the door. "You're all I want," she said, looking into Gi's blue eyes. "I love you, Gianna Revisi. You and only you."

Gi closed the distance between them, shoving Taren against the wall with a searing kiss as she began pulling her clothes away in haste, nearly ripping them as love and anger-fueled passion burned between them.

Taren wanted nothing more than to get naked and make love with Gi right there on the cold tile floor of the foyer, but she pushed her away enough to part their hungry mouths.

"Wait," she said breathlessly. "There's another reason I'm here," she added, licking the traces of their frantic kissing from her lips.

"I don't care," Gi replied, quieting her with another deep kiss.

Clothes were tossed and reality forgotten as they crashed onto the couch, fervently touching each other. Their lips traded bruising kisses as their hands worked back and forth, giving and taking what they wanted from the other.

"Come with me," Taren hissed between kisses, barely able to hold on as the fire in her belly moved lower.

Gi moved further over her as they began panting and moaning together in the throes of passion. The added weight on the edge of the couch caused them to topple over, winding up in a heap of nakedness on the hard floor as the last of their climax drifted away.

"Wow," Taren murmured, stirring first.

Gi untangled herself slowly as she came down from the intoxicating high. She peered down at the woman next to her.

"What the hell was that?" Taren asked.

"I imagine it's called hate sex," Gi replied.

Taren nodded as she pushed herself into a sitting position. "So, you hate me? Or we hate each other? How does that work?"

Gi leaned her back against the couch and glared at her. "I could never hate you, tesoro." She shook her head. "I hate how in love I am with you; how in love I've been since the first time I kissed you."

"Why do you hate it?" Taren whispered, grabbing her hand.

"Because my love isn't enough for you," Gi sighed.

"Gianna, I want nothing more than to be with you," Taren said.

Gi looked at her strangely. She almost never used Gi's full first name.

"I left you in college because a criminal lifestyle wasn't what I wanted and you couldn't let it go." Taren shook her head. "I knew when I saw you at Rapture that it wouldn't be long before I was back in your arms. My chest ached every time I thought about you. I couldn't sleep, Gi, I never stopped loving you. I just tried to make myself forget."

"What happens now?" Gi asked, gently brushing the long locks from Taren's face.

"I don't know. I want to be with you, Gi, to live my life with you, but you may hate me when I tell you the other reason why I'm here." She knew how difficult it was for Gi to trust anyone, so she wondered how she was going to react to her own flesh and blood embezzling millions from her.

"I doubt that, unless you're pregnant," Gi replied, raising an eyebrow.

"Oh, God no." Taren shook her head. "Can we maybe get off the floor and—"

"Have a little decency?" Gi laughed.

"Something like that." Taren smiled.

After redressing, Gi and Taren sat together in the den upstairs.

"I love this room. It's my favorite," Taren said, sinking into the soft leather cushions.

"Mine, too." Gi put her feet up on the ottoman and crossed her ankles. "So, what's the real reason that brought you to my doorstep?"

"You mean besides me packing my belongings into two suitcases and driving over here on a hope and a prayer?" Taren laughed softly. "I was so pissed at you, and I wanted to prove you were lying to me about the business being completely legal because you kept brushing me off when I came to you with the variances."

"What did you do?" Gi asked, furrowing her brow.

"My passwords still worked in the system, so I didn't really hack into anything. I simply dug a lot deeper. Anyway," Taren took a deep breath. "Gi, your Uncle Bruno is extorting money from you and using Gentlemen's Rook to hide it. I'm surprised you haven't figured this out. You're the smartest person I know, and you were basically doing everything alone until you brought me into the picture. What I don't understand is why you even trusted him in the first place. You always told me never to trust anyone, not even family."

Gi turned her head, staring at the wall on the other side of the room.

"Tell me I didn't uncover something bad, Gi." Taren grabbed her hand.

Gi let out a long breath and shook her head. "Just let it go, please?"

"What do you mean, let it go?" Taren asked, pulling her hand away.

"Just this once, it's best if you don't know what's going on, tesoro."

"Don't you dare call me that. Not when you're hiding something from me. Damn it!" Taren yelled.

"Calm down," Gi consoled her. The look in Taren's eyes tore her apart.

Taren moved to stand up and Gi grabbed her hand, holding her close. "Let me go," Taren warned.

"I know about everything," Gi sighed. "I know…because I set it up," she added, hanging her head.

"Set what up? What's going on?" Taren turned towards her.

"Bruno's in trouble with the FBI." Gi bit her lower lip and shrugged. "I'm helping them bust him."

"You're what?!?" Taren exclaimed.

"You know my family history with the Outfit. Bruno tried desperately to join them, but after years of being rejected, he started his own operation. I wasn't aware of anything until the FBI came to me." Gi looked at the shocked expression on Taren's face. "You looked about like I did when they told me he'd been in major contact with large, international prostitution rings and traffickers."

"Are you serious?"

Gi nodded. "He's made a few friends in high places. Anyway, his multiple international trips flagged him and they began looking into his background. I had no idea. I guess it all started sometime after my father passed. By the time I'd opened R&R, he'd made a lot of high profile connections."

"How the hell did he wind up working with you?"

"He came to me with the business plan for GR. He was looking for a way to have a legacy for his sons and the family name. At least, that's the line of bullshit he fed me. You know I don't trust anyone, so I wasn't going to do it, but apparently his sudden involvement with me sent the FBI on my trail. They tore through my financial records, but of course found nothing but a legitimate business."

Taren shook her head. "That's insane."

"It gets better. They interviewed me about my time in Paris and Milan, trying to make a connection to him, I guess. I mentioned how I'd really only seen him during the holidays, especially since my father had passed, but he came to me with the business plan recently. That's when they told me everything that he'd been up to. I was floored, first that he was smart of enough to run a crime operation, and second that he was stupid enough to get involved with prostitution and sex trafficking."

"I feel disgusted to have ever been in the same room as him," Taren shivered.

"How do you think I feel? He's my damn flesh and blood!" Gi shook her head. "I told them I'd cooperate and do whatever they wanted in order to take him down. They asked me to go along with the business, so I did." Gi shrugged. "Apparently, he's extorted a couple million dollars from me, which he doesn't think I know about, and used it to pay these foreign crime organizations to get the women over here."

"What's he doing with them?"

"They're working in the bar as waitresses, but each one has a calling card, so to speak. When one of them asks for a certain type of whiskey or cigar, he's actually paying for a particular woman and the number of drinks or cigars he buys is the number of hours he has with her."

"Like a prostitute?" Taren grimaced.

"Yes, but these women are being forced into this as sex slaves."

"Oh, my God!"

"Taren, this thing involves way more people than I ever realized. The mayor, the governor, and a congressman are on the VIP list. That's actually why I've been spending so much time with Valerie, the mayor's assistant."

Taren raised an eyebrow.

"She's an undercover FBI agent and one of the lead investigators on this case. That's how we've been passing information back and forth."

"Where do I fit into all of this?"

Gi sighed. "I never planned on seeing you again, and then you walked into my bar. When you showed up again as my accountant, I had to bring you in close to me. I couldn't handle something happening to you during all of this. Valerie was already having an issue keeping the records for everything Bruno was doing, and the guy you replaced was a damn buffoon. I knew you'd be able to put everything into a nice, neat order, and I wanted to make sure you were safe, so I brought you in."

"Did you ever plan on telling me?"

Gi bit her lower lip. "Honestly, I don't know. You were with Ken and I just wanted to know you were safe. I didn't think we'd wind up having an affair."

"Yeah, me either." Taren shook her head. "So, if all this was going on, why not tell me? Why did you let me go on thinking you were doing something illegal again?"

"I didn't want you involved. That's why I brushed it aside every time you came to me. No one in this entire company knows, except me…and now you."

"Why did I still have access to everything after I quit?"

"Because Valerie is close to closing the case and I didn't want anything to look suspicious. Everyone thinks your grandmother is sick again and that's where you went so abruptly. I had to keep you in the system." Gi smiled. "I know you're smart—and a little too damn good at your job, if you ask me—but I never thought you'd continue snooping after I ended everything."

Taren laughed. "I was so mad. I wanted to prove you wrong."

"Yeah, I figured as much when I saw you logging into different accounts, but I didn't expect you'd put it all together. I thought you'd give up after a couple of days."

"Did you deliberately push me away?" Taren asked, squeezing her hand.

"Yes and no," Gi replied. "I didn't want you to be a physical part of all this when it went down. I wanted you innocent. At the same time, I knew I was still in love with you the moment I sat down in front of you at Rapture that first night, plus I hated the fact that you were with someone else, and a man to boot." Gi pulled Taren's hand up, kissing the back of it softly. "I'm sorry I pulled you into all of this, tesoro."

"Don't be. There's nowhere that I'd rather be. You're doing the right thing by stopping him." Taren kissed Gi's cheek before asking, "Are Sergio and Mario involved with this mess?"

"As far as I know. They're all connected."

"That's sad that he's going to take his own children down with him."

Gi shrugged. "He raised them to think they were true gangsters. My dad was smarter. He refused when the Outfit came calling. He chose his wife and kid."

"If your dad wasn't in the mob, how did you wind up doing what you did?"

"I guess it skipped a generation," she said.

"Uh huh," Taren laughed.

"The gambling ring started as a couple of parties and grew into a full-blown underground business. My dealings in Paris and Milan were simply because I knew how to do it, and I knew it would make money fast. But you know that."

Taren nodded. "So, where does this leave us, now that I know?"

"You're going to have to go back to work like you were just out of town. You have to act like nothing has changed, especially around the office because it's wired."

The colored drained from Taren's face as she began remembering things that happened between she and Gi at the office, including conversations about their past.

"It's okay. They're not looking at me. They've already done that, remember? Besides, I've been clean since I left Milan and nothing I have ever done can be traced to me. One thing I was good at was being a successful crime boss."

"Yeah." Taren grinned, shaking her head. "If you knew the place was bugged, why didn't you stop me when things got physical?"

"I was so caught up in being close to you again, I forgot about them. They'd already been there for almost two months, and it slipped my mind."

"You didn't get questioned about our affair? Wait, let me guess, it wasn't the first time." Taren pursed her lips.

Gi smiled. "Why do you think I've had all of these women?"

"Have you looked in a mirror lately?" Taren chided. "You're the walking, talking poster girl for sex appeal. If I'd never met you until that night at Rapture, I'd have been drawn to you in more ways than one. You're mysterious, smart, sexy, and dangerous. It's a wicked combination," She winked.

Gi burst with laughter. "You're a mess, you know that? No, I don't have women throwing themselves at my feet. Yes, I've dated here and there, but nothing serious. Yes, I've had sex in the office, but only one other time and that was way before all of this. And no, I've never loved anyone except you."

"You know, girls used to come up to me all the time in college, asking about you and telling me they knew someone who dated you."

"I had a few years on you in college. So yeah, I may have dated a little, but I can count on both hands how many people I've slept with and still have fingers left over. They were doing it to get to you. You had the girl everyone wanted." Gi grinned.

"You better stop before your head gets too big for this room," Taren teased.

Gi moved swiftly, pushing Taren to her back on the couch as she moved on top of her, kissing her softly. "Shouldn't we discuss…" A few more delicate kisses. "Things like closet space and…which side of the bed you want?"

"We managed living together in that tiny apartment with no problem, I'm sure we'll figure it out." Taren paused. "That is if you want me here. I could always go—"

"You're not going anywhere," Gi mumbled grinding their hips together.

"I love you," Taren whispered, before pulling her down for a heated kiss.

# Chapter 24

The following day, Taren walked into the office and pretended she hadn't moved in with Gi the night before. Everything appeared the same, like she'd stepped out of time for the past week.

"How's your grandmother?" Gi's assistant asked, passing her in the hallway.

"She's much better, thanks," Taren replied as she poured a fresh cup of coffee. She headed back to her office. She had a stack of new invoices to put into the system and another stack of bills to pay, plus she had to do the reporting for the end of the month. Thankfully, it was enough busy work to keep her mind off the reality of everything rolling around in her thoughts.

By the middle of the day, she'd nearly forgotten about everything, until Gi waltzed into her office.

"Hey." Taren smiled.

"Have you had lunch yet?" Gi asked, quietly kissing her cheek.

"I haven't had time. I can't believe how much work piled up while I was gone."

"Yeah, seems we can't figure out how to pay the bills without you," Gi teased. "Come on, let me buy you lunch."

Taren went to protest, knowing she wanted to get a bigger dent in her workload before she left for the day, but

Gi was nodding towards the door like she had some kind of nervous problem.

"Okay, but I get to pick the place."

\*\*\*

As soon as they were in Gi's car, Taren leaned over the center console and kissed her hard.

"What was that for?" Gi asked, when she pulled away to buckle her seatbelt.

Taren shrugged and smiled. "I felt like kissing you."

"Well, I feel like sliding my—"

"Drive us to lunch, Revisi!" Taren chided with a laughed. "Sushi sounds good right about now."

Gi shook her head, wanting to make another comment. "I just got a text message from Valerie. Uncle Bruno is out of the country at the moment."

"What's he doing?"

"Shopping for more women, I guess. He told me he was going on a golfing trip with Congressman Brown. That sorry piece of shit has never swung a club in his life, so I knew something was up. She said he arrived two days ago and has a return trip booked for next Monday."

"Where are Sergio and Mario?"

"Sergio is in charge of the bar, I assume. This is inventory week, so Mario has been at Rogue and Rapture."

Gi pulled into a Japanese restaurant parking lot and shut the car off. "Valerie said they're going to wait for him to bring the women into the bar, and then bust the entire operation. I only have a couple of days to expedite all the paperwork to put Gentlemen's Rook in Uncle Bruno's name."

"Wow, they're moving in that fast?"

"Yeah. When we get back to the office, I need you to change all of the GR bank accounts, vendor accounts, everything to his name. I'm going to the courthouse when I drop you off to get the business license changed. I just faxed all the paperwork to the IRS and the State of Illinois, removing my name and any association with R&R Enterprises."

"When will that take effect?"

"As soon as they get the papers and input it. Valerie assured me it would be completed by Monday. She made a few calls to be sure. Everything has to be in his name before they can make their move, or I go down with his sinking ship."

"That's cutting it close, isn't it?"

"He'll be back sometime Monday afternoon, and then he'll probably get the girls in on Wednesday. He won't notice anything between now and then with the accounts, so we'll be good."

"Let's eat in a hurry then. I have a lot to do when I get back."

\*\*\*

When the weekend arrived, Taren and Gi spent the entire two days wrapped in each other's arms. They made love in between watching movies and eating their meals, but mostly just enjoyed being together. Taren felt different this time around. There was nothing between them, pushing them in opposite directions. Soon, the mess with Bruno would be behind them as well. She looked forward to having a completely blank slate for their new start.

Sydney Canyon

On Sunday evening, they were watching some romantic comedy that Gi was vaguely interested in, but she had Taren in her arms and that was all that mattered to her.

"Were you really planning on marrying Ken? I mean, would you have gone through with it?" she asked, holding Taren close.

"I don't know, probably not. Deep down I think I knew it wasn't where I was meant to be," Taren answered, kissing her softly.

"Would you marry me?"

Taren stiffened and sat up a little to look into Gi's eyes. "Are you proposing?"

Realizing how the question sounded, Gi shook her head. "That's not really how I envisioned it, no, but is it something you've thought about?"

Taren smiled. "Of course. I thought about it when we were in college and the day he asked me, I actually thought about you."

"Then why did you say yes?"

"Gi, I'd started a new life and I was trying really hard to make it work. Having a life with him seemed like the right thing to do," she sighed. "All I've been doing since college is trying to get over you. Nothing worked for long. You always found a way back into my dreams."

"That's because you needed to get under me, not over me," Gi teased, breaking the icy conversation.

Taren rolled her eyes as she reached for the remote, clicking the TV off.

"What are you doing?" Gi asked. "I thought you were dying to see this movie?"

"I was, but getting under sounds like a much better idea," she replied, wrapping her arms around Gi and pulling her down.

# Chapter 25

The following Wednesday started like any other. Gi was in her office, working on the new advertising campaign, and Taren was in hers, working on the ledger for the new month. It wasn't until later in the afternoon that Gi got the call that the FBI had busted down the door of Gentlemen's Rook and swarmed the building, arresting Bruno, Sergio, and Mario, along with all of their staff, including the women, who turned out to be victims who thought they had no rights. Of course, Gi had to act like she wasn't involved at first. She ran into Taren's office, telling her everything, like they knew nothing about it. Then, she called her lawyer to let him know what had happened. She sent him copies of all of the paperwork, transferring everything over to Bruno, which was in their original business plan on file with his office. She knew she wasn't going to be arrested or even investigated, but she had to pretend as if she were because of their connection and her involvement with starting the business. Her lawyer made a few calls and told her to say nothing and have him contacted immediately if they showed up.

Everything had gone as Valerie had said it would. Bruno and the boys had held a staff meeting to introduce the new girls, which meant all of the employees were there, but he'd also invited a handful of his top clients, including the mayor, the governor, the congressman, and two corporate CEOs, all of whom were arrested when the place was raided.

As Valerie promised, no one came after Gi, despite Bruno ranting and raving that the entire thing was Gianna Revisi's idea from the start. Knowing she was finally free and clear of everything, Gi put the business up for sale since she had no interest in it to begin with.

Later that evening, as they watched the story on the local news, Gi felt a wave of relief. She hated keeping the secrets, but most of all, she hated knowing what he was doing and having to wait for the feds to bust him. She wanted to rip his head off and kick it down the street.

"Do you think we're going to have a news crew camped out in front of the office tomorrow?" Taren asked.

Gi gestured towards the front of the house. "They arrived while you were in the shower. My lawyer gave my statement already. I have no reason to talk to anyone. I wasn't involved and my uncle just extorted millions of dollars from me to sell women as sex slaves. I think I deserve my privacy."

Taren nodded. "Good point."

"I feel bad for my family though. Bruno, Sergio, and Mario are going to prison. All that is left is me and my mother."

"Bruno wasn't married?"

"No. His wife divorced him ages ago because she'd had enough. He always had a piece of ass on the side anyway." She said.

"Will I get to meet your mom soon?" Taren asked.

"Yeah, when she gets back. I put her on a plane to Italy a week ago to visit her sister for a month. She does this every year about this time, so it was nothing new to her, but I didn't want her here when this shit went down." Gi looked at the clock. "She probably won't hear anything where she is, so I'll have to call her."

"I should probably call my family as well. They know I work for you, and well, they know we're together."

"They do?" Gi raised an eyebrow.

"Yes. I had to tell them Ken and I split up because he'll be dropping off my stuff at their house when he cleans out the storage shed we shoved all of our shit into when we moved out here."

"I had no idea you'd called. How did it go?"

"I called them Saturday when you fell asleep." Taren smiled, remembering what had put Gi to sleep like a baby. "My parents just want to see me happy, but I think they were in shock. I'm sure this is going to drive their anxiety level up a little bit. They were all for me and Ken getting married. They never knew about you, so they think I'm nervous about getting married and this is a phase, or something."

"Maybe we should book a trip to San Diego when things settle down. If they meet me and see us together, maybe they will have a better understanding."

"Melanie's going to flip out. When I went home to see my grandmother, Ken was blabbing to my father about my new job and he mentioned your name. She overheard and drilled me about being back around you. I thought I was going to have to turn the hose on her."

Gi rolled her eyes. "She tried her damndest to break us up in college. I'm sure she was strutting like a rooster when you left me."

Taren laughed. "She's married now with two kids and has her own issues. Besides, our little conversation made me question a lot of things, which is why I came straight to you when I got back."

Gi grinned. "I'm sure she'd love to know that." She was about say something else when her cell phone rang. She quickly answered, saying only a few words before hanging up.

Taren looked at her with a questioning expression.

"That was Valerie. The arraignment hearing is in the morning."

"Are you going?"

"Probably. He threw my name up all day in questioning, even when his lawyer told him to be quiet. She said he's pissed."

"Good. He's a piece of shit," Taren spat.

"I'm sick of talking about family," Gi sighed.

"Me too," Taren agreed, running her hand through Gi's short hair. "I love you so damn much."

"I love you, too, tesoro." Gi smiled, pulling Taren close and wrapping her arms around her. "I missed this," she murmured, curling up with her.

# *Epilogue*

"Are you ready for this?" Taren asked, before they opened the doors to the courtroom.

It had been eight months since Bruno, Sergio, and Mario were arrested, and after ten weeks of trial, including testimony from Gi, all three of them were found guilty and set to be sentenced today.

"I'm ready to put all this behind me," Gi replied, grabbing her hand.

They walked in together, taking their seats directly behind the federal prosecutor's table. Gi didn't have to look to her left where her three family members sat with their team of lawyers; she felt their cold hard stares on the side of her face.

"All rise for the Honorable Judge Mary Worthington," the bailiff said loudly.

"Here we go," Gi whispered as she stood.

The judge walked into the room and took a seat. She looked out at everyone in the room and said, "You may be seated."

Gi's heart raced. She was angry for being betrayed by her own flesh and blood, but she was more disgusted with what they were doing, and hoped the judge saw through the lies told during the trial.

The judge asked the defendants to stand. Then she put her reading glasses on and read a statute number, along with each charge they were found guilty of.

"Bruno Revisi, Sergio Revisi, and Mario Revisi, the United States Federal Court hereby sentences each of you to a prison term of twenty years for human trafficking for sexual exploitation; three years for keeping a brothel used for prostitution; and two years for exploitation of prostitution, all of which are to be served consecutively and without the option of early parole," she stated, dropping the gavel.

When the bailiff moved to escort the men out of the room, Bruno jumped up and shouted at Gi. "You fucking nark! You shame the Revisi name! *Pezzo di merda!*"

It took three officers to pull Bruno away from the banister separating the two of them.

"The shame is yours!" She stepped closer to him. "You and your sons are the only Revisis to ever get caught with your hands dirty and wind up in prison," she added, shaking her head.

"Fuck you!" he shouted as they began dragging him away.

"No, you tried that, but you got fucked instead! Trust no one, not even your own flesh and blood," she spat, before grabbing Taren's hand and walking away.

\*\*\*

When they got home, Taren removed her skirt and blouse, placing them neatly in the space across from Gi's where the rest of her clothes were hanging.

"I feel like a huge weight has been lifted off me," Gi said as she began removing her pantsuit. She put her jacket on a hanger in the closet, and then tossed her blouse into the dry-cleaning pile, having smeared it with nervous sweat during the hearing. She walked over to the chaise by the fireplace, and sat down to remove her socks and shoes.

"Why do you think Bruno did it?" Taren asked, walking closer to her.

"He wanted to be a gangster. But you don't become a crime boss by fucking people over, especially another crime boss," Gi stated.

Taren put her hand on Gi's shoulder, pushing her to her back as she straddled her lap. "Fucking a crime boss sounds like a great idea right about now," she declared, leaning down and kissing her hard.

# About the Author

Sydney enjoys reading everything from magazines to historical books and boasts about her massive collection of paperbacks and hardbacks in her personal library. She's also a huge fan of multiple TV shows, which she says take up too much of her time. She enjoys writing novellas and is the author of the bestselling novellas: *One Night* and *Shadow's Eyes*. *Second Chance* was her first full length, printed novel.

You can message her and like her fan page at
facebook.com/sydneycanyon

**visit us at www.tri-pub.com**

## Other Titles Available From
## Triplicity Publishing

***Second Chance*** by Sydney Canyon. After an attack on her convoy, Marine Corps Staff Sergeant, Darien Hollister, must learn to live without her sight. When an experimental procedure allows her to see again, Darien is torn, knowing someone had to die in order for this to happen. She embarks on a journey to personally thank the donor's family, but is too stunned to tell them the truth. When the truth finally comes out, Darien walks away, taking the second chance that she's been given to go back to the only life she's ever known, but she's not the only one with a second chance at life.

***Meant to Be*** by Graysen Morgen. Brandt is about to walk down the aisle with her girlfriend, when an unexpected chain of events turns her world upside down, causing her to question the last three years of her life. A chance encounter sparks a mix of rage and excitement that she has never felt before. Summer is living life and following her dreams, all the while, harboring a huge secret that could ruin her career. She believes that some things are better kept in the dark, until she has her third run-in with a woman she had hoped to never see again, and gives into temptation. Brandt and Summer start believing everything happens for a reason as they learn the true meaning of *meant to be*.

***Coming Home*** by Graysen Morgen. After tragedy derails TJ Abernathy's life, she packs up her three year old son and heads back to Pennsylvania to live with her grandmother on the family farm. TJ picks back up where she left off eight years earlier, tending to the fruit and nut tree orchard, while learning her grandmother's secret trade. Soon, TJ's high school sweetheart and the same girl who broke her heart, comes back into her life, threatening to steal it away once again. As the weeks turn into months and tragedy strikes again, TJ realizes coming home was the best thing she could've ever done.

***Special Assignment*** by Austen Thorne. Secret Service Agent Parker Meeks has her hands full when she gets her new assignment, protecting a Congressman's teenage daughter, who has had threats made on her life and been whisked away to a Christian boarding school under an alias to finish out her senior year. Parker is fine with the assignment, until she finds out she has to go undercover as a Canon Priest. The last thing Parker expects to find is a beautiful, art history teacher, who is intrigued by her in more ways than one.

***Miracle at Christmas*** by Sydney Canyon. A Modern Twist on the Classic Scrooge Story. Dylan is a power-hungry lawyer who pushed away everything good in her life to become the best defense attorney in the, often winning the worst cases and keeping anyone with enough money out of jail. She's visited on Christmas Eve by her deceased law partner, who threatens her with a life in hell like his own, if she doesn't change her path. During the course of the night, she is taken on a journey through her past, present, and future with three very different spirits.

***Bella Vita*** by Sydney Canyon. Brady is the First Officer of the crew on the *Bella Vita*, a luxury charter yacht in the Caribbean. She enjoys the laidback island lifestyle, and is accustomed to high profile guests, but when a U.S. Senator charters the yacht as a gift to his beautiful twin daughters who have just graduated from college and a few of their friends, she literally has her hands full.

***Brides*** *(Bridal Series book 2)* by Graysen Morgen. Britton Prescott is dating the love of her life, Daphne Attwood, after a few tumultuous events that happened to unravel at her sister's wedding reception, seven months earlier. She's happy with the way things are, but immense pressure from her family and friends to take the next step, nearly sends her back to the single life. The idea of a long engagement and simple wedding are thrown out the window, as both families take over, rushing Britton and Daphne to the altar in a matter of weeks.

***Cypress Lake*** by Graysen Morgen. The small town of Cypress Lake is rocked when one murder after another happens. Dani Ricketts, the Chief Deputy for the Cypress Lake Sheriff's Office, realizes the murders are linked. She's surprised when the girl that broke her heart in high school has not only returned home, but she's also Dani's only suspect. Kristen Malone has come back to Cypress Lake to put the past behind her so that she can move on with her life. Seeing Dani Ricketts again throws her off-guard, nearly derailing her plans to finally rid herself and her family of Cypress Lake.

***Crashing Waves*** by Graysen Morgen. After a tragic accident, Pro Surfer, Rory Eden, spends her days hiding in the surf and snowboard manufacturing company that she built from the ground up, while living her life as a shell of the person that she once was. Rory's world is turned upside when a young surfer pursues her, asking for the one thing she can't do. Adler Troy and Dr. Cason Macauley from Graysen Morgen's best seller, *Falling Snow,* make an appearance in this romantic adventure about life, love, and letting go.

***Bridesmaid of Honor*** *(Bridal Series book 1)* by Graysen Morgen. Britton Prescott's best friend is getting married and she's the maid of honor. As if that isn't enough to deal with, Britton's sister announces she's getting married in the same month and her maid of honor is her best friend Daphne, the same woman who has tormented Britton for years. Britton has to suck it up and play nice, instead of scratching her eyes out, because she and Daphne are in both weddings. Everyone is counting on them to behave like adults.

***Falling Snow*** by Graysen Morgen. Dr. Cason Macauley, a high-speed trauma surgeon from Denver meets Adler Troy, a professional snowboarder and sparks fly. The last thing Cason wants is a relationship and Adler doesn't realize what's right in front of her until it's gone, but will it be too late?

***Fate vs. Destiny*** by Graysen Morgen. Logan Greer devotes her life to investigating plane crashes for the National Transportation Safety Board. Brooke McCabe is an investigator with the Federal Aviation Association who literally flies by the seat of her pants. When Logan gets tangled in head games with both women will she choose fate or destiny?

***Just Me*** by Graysen Morgen. Wild child Ian Wiley has to grow up and take the reins of the hundred year old family business when tragedy strikes. Cassidy Harland is a little surprised that she came within an inch of picking up a gorgeous stranger in a bar and is shocked to find out that stranger is the new head of her company.

*Love Loss Revenge* by Graysen Morgen. Rian Casey is an FBI Agent working the biggest case of her career and madly in love with her girlfriend. Her world is turned upside when tragedy strikes. Heartbroken, she tries to rebuild her life. When she discovers the truth behind what really happened that awful night she decides justice isn't good enough, and vows revenge on everyone involved.

*Natural Instinct* by Graysen Morgen. Chandler Scott is a Marine Biologist who keeps her private life private. Corey Joslen is intrigued by Chandler from the moment she meets her. Chandler is forced to finally open her life up to Corey. It backfires in Corey's face and sends her running. Will either woman learn to trust her natural instinct?

*Secluded Heart* by Graysen Morgen. Chase Leery is an overworked cardiac surgeon with a group of best friends that have an opinion and a reason for everything. When she meets a new artist named Remy Sheridan at her best friend's art gallery she is captivated by the reclusive woman. When Chase finds out why Remy is so sheltered will she put her career on the line to help her or is it too difficult to love someone with a secluded heart?

*In Love, at War* by Graysen Morgen. Charley Hayes is in the Army Air Force and stationed at Ford Island in Pearl Harbor. She is the commanding officer of her own female-only service squadron and doing the one thing she loves most, repairing airplanes. Life is good for Charley, until the day she finds herself falling in love while fighting for her life as her country is thrown haphazardly into World War II. Can she survive being in love and at war?

***Fast Pitch*** by Graysen Morgen. Graham Cahill is a senior in college and the catcher and captain of the softball team. Despite being an all-star pitcher, Bailey Michaels is young and arrogant. Graham and Bailey are forced to get to know each other off the field in order to learn to work together on the field. Will the extra time pay off or will it drive a nail through the team?

***Submerged*** by Graysen Morgen. Assistant District Attorney Layne Carmichael had no idea that the sexy woman she took home from a local bar for a one night stand would turn out to be someone she would be prosecuting months later. Scooter is a Naval Officer on a submarine who changes women like she changes uniforms. When she is accused of a heinous crime she is shocked to see her latest conquest sitting across from her as the prosecuting attorney.

***Vow of Solitude*** by Austen Thorne. Detective Jordan Denali is in a fight for her life against the ghosts from her past and a Serial Killer taunting her with his every move. She lives a life of solitude and plans to keep it that way. When Callie Marceau, a curious Medical Examiner, decides she wants in on the biggest case of her career, as well as, Jordan's life, Jordan is powerless to stop her.

***Igniting Temptation*** by Sydney Canyon. Mackenzie Trotter is the Head of Pediatrics at the local hospital. Her life takes a rather unexpected turn when she meets a flirtatious, beautiful fire fighter. Both women soon discover it doesn't take much to ignite temptation.

*One Night* by Sydney Canyon. While on a business trip, Caylen Jarrett spends an amazing night with a beautiful stripper. Months later, she is shocked and confused when that same woman re-enters her life. The fact that this stranger could destroy her career doesn't bother her. C.J. is more terrified of the feelings this woman stirs in her. Could she have fallen in love in one night and not even known it?

*Fine* by Sydney Can

yon. Collin Anderson hides behind a façade, pretending everything is fine. Her workaholic wife and best friend are both oblivious as she goes on an emotional journey, battling a potentially hereditary disease that her mother has been diagnosed with. The only person who knows what is really going on, is Collin's doctor. The same doctor, who is an acquaintance that she's always been attracted to, and who has a partner of her own.

*Shadow's Eyes* by Sydney Canyon. Tyler McCain is the owner of a large ranch that breeds and sells different types of horses. She isn't exactly thrilled when a Hollywood movie producer shows up wanting to film his latest movie on her property. Reegan Delsol is an up and coming actress who has everything going for her when she lands the lead role in a new film, but there one small problem that could blow the entire picture.

**Light Reading: A Collection of Novellas** by Sydney Canyon. Four of Sydney Canyon's novellas together in one book, including the bestsellers *Shadow's Eyes* and *One Night*.

*Sydney Canyon*

**Visit us at www.tri-pub.com**